DISAPPEARANCE

Also by David Dabydeen

Fiction:
The Intended
The Counting House
A Harlot's Progress
Our Lady of Demerara
Molly and the Muslim Stick
Johnson's Dictionary

Poetry:
Slave Song
Coolie Odyssey
Turner

Non-fiction:
Hogarth's Blacks: Images of Blacks in Eighteenth Century English Art
Hogarth, Walpole and Commercial Britain
Paks Brittanica

DAVID DABYDEEN

DISAPPEARANCE

PEEPAL TREE

First published in Great Britain in 1993
by Secker & Warburg

This revised edition published in 2005
Reprinted 2013
Peepal Tree Press Ltd
17 King's Avenue
Leeds LS6 1QS
England

ISBN 9781845230142

 Peepal Tree gratefully acknowledges Arts Council support

For Susy Diamond (d. 1991) and

Margaret Niland (d. 1991),

and for Frances, Dinah, Jill and Luke Winch

All at once he leaned down and splashed the liquid
extravagantly on his face to clear away all doubt of
a concrete existence.

Wilson Harris, *The Secret Ladder*

Was it Jack? I didn't take the person in; I was more
concerned with the strangeness of the walk, my own
strangeness, and the absurdity of my enquiry.

V. S. Naipaul, *The Enigma of Arrival*

Mistah Kurtz – he dead.

T. S. Eliot, *The Hollow Men*

What opens meaning and language is writing as the
disappearance of natural presence.

Jacques Derrida, *Of Grammatology*

Rejoice! Rejoice!

Margaret Thatcher

PART I

ONE

Why, Mrs Rutherford wanted to know, did I become an engineer? She sat on her rocking chair overlooking a garden which ran down to the edge of Dunsmere Cliff and a sheer drop of ninety feet. I sat with her each afternoon after work, fielding questions about the state of the cliff – the progress of our efforts to save it tumbling into the sea together with twelve or thirteen houses (including hers), the drift of shingle from Hastings' beach, whether another landslip was imminent and if so what I intended to do about it – and dozens of others. Generalised answers were not sufficient. She wanted details and seemed to have a mind unbearably patient and capable of absorbing the minutest fragments of information. I admired her curiosity and once told her so – after much hesitation, in case she thought I was being patronising. 'It's the way of the desert,' she said plainly, without the faintest hint of mysteriousness in her voice.

She left me alone for the first hour, when I would come home weary of the day's calculations, inspections and mishaps. I went to my room, showered and put on the freshly laundered clothes she had laid out on the bed. I wore whatever she decided to leave out and she in turn was pleased to see me in her choice of shirt. When I took lodgings with her she had offered to do my laundry, taking pity as she saw me bend over the board, ironing only the front and cuffs of my shirts to save time. I gladly handed over my wardrobe to her care, and she quickly discarded the shirts she took a dislike to, because of their coarse sewing or design, and secreted them in my suitcase at the bottom of the bed. She went to the shops and bought more civilised replacements. Although in her sixties, she seemed to have a keen eye for fashion, as the ties she made me wear sometimes drew admiring glances from my colleagues on the beach. I suppose it made her feel that she was back with her husband, though I was thirty years younger than her, and from a different culture. I could imagine her relishing the gossip of the village, the old folk not having a scandal to exercise their tongues for decades. As it was, she was already the odd one out among the inhabitants, the one who had lived in Africa and whose husband had abandoned her childless. And it was she who, refusing to surrender to fat and the sagging skin of old age, took up running with the Hastings Harriers, an amateur club of mostly middle-aged businessmen for whom squash was now too dangerous. Every Thursday and Sunday she ran four miles with them, through fields or along paths that skirted the cliff-top. Her pace was deliberate, she frequently paused to look at foxgloves or bluebells which she swore were not there the last time she ran that way. And she always came in last, holding up the minibus which took the club back to the various villages dotted around Hastings.

In the second hour I took tea with her. An assortment of cakes and preserves, neatly arranged on the dining-table, greeted me when I came downstairs. A faint afternoon sun lit up part of the African batik covering the table. She sat opposite me eating slowly, a faraway look on her face. Behind her was a row of shelves bearing wooden and clay pots she had brought back from her travels in the 1950s and '60s.

It was only in the third hour, after she had cleared the table, directing me to the sitting-room, that she would talk in earnest. She brought glasses of damson wine and encouraged me to light up. 'Of course I don't mind,' she said the first time I asked permission to smoke, rifling through drawers to find an ashtray. 'I like the smell of tobacco.' At the first hint of smoke she twitched her nose pleasurably but then coughed. 'I've forgotten how long it's been since a man breathed smoke in this room... twenty years ago perhaps... around 1972... August, yes August.' It was always thus with her – an initial fuzziness, as if she didn't want to remember, then, the process of recollection begun, a startling exactitude. 'It was Jack, my husband. He fumbled in his pouch and refused to look me in the eye. He lit a cigarette and hid behind a cloud of smoke while mumbling something about how he'd

12

leave me money. You know how magicians disappear in a puff of smoke? He must have been planning some equally mysterious exit because he blew a puff in my direction thinking I'd be blinded and he could make for the door quickly, leaving me all perplexed. But I knew all along he'd be leaving, the foolish man.'

'Where did he go to?' I asked hesitantly, not wishing to sound too inquisitive.

'Oh, somewhere or other, I never bothered to enquire.' Her voice trailed off for a moment before recovering to confront me with an unfathomable question. 'Where do men go to when they leave their wives?'

'To other women,' I answered automatically, recalling the infidelity of my own father.

'Not Jack. As soon as the door closed behind him I knew he was going to his grave. There was too much longing and guilt in him for a proper life.'

'Have you never been intrigued about what became of him?' I persisted.

'I banked the cheque, that's all, and forgot him,' she replied, in such a decisive tone that I knew she intended to end my enquiries abruptly. 'August 6th – that's the last I saw of him. Late afternoon I'd say, about this time of the day. He sat exactly where you're sitting now.' I shifted uncomfortably in the chair. 'He cried. I forgave him, as he knew I would.'

It was with the same precision of timing that she would begin our early-evening sessions. Satisfied that I was bathed and re-freshed, and waiting until I was half-way into the cigarette, she would open with a technical question relating to the cliff before nudging the conversation around to the personal. Once, as she sat rocking, staring out of the window as if formulating the evening's dialogue, I startled her with a pre-emptive question.

'How old are all these pots?' I asked innocently, pointing to the shelves by the dining-table.

She fumbled for speech, then quickly recomposed her mind. 'It's impossible to tell. The Pende and Yaka tribes have been making such pots for hundreds of years. I bought them in a market in Dakar though, so it's difficult to identify them precisely in terms of age or tribal style.'

I looked sheepish, unable to follow up with a comment or gesture, not even a nod signifying vague knowledge of the geography. 'Dakar is the capital of Senegal, in West Africa. It's thousands of miles from where the Pende and Yaka live, in the Congo, so the pots are unlikely to have travelled that far west.' She got up, walked heavily over to the shelves (by evening, the strength drained from her limbs and she grew visibly frail and elderly) and brought back two wooden pots. 'This one looks like a Yaka carving,' she said, holding it up to the light so that I could get a clearer view. I leant forward and looked hard and ignorantly at it. The pot was shaped as a female figure, and a particularly crude one at that, with stiff protruding breasts like the tips of fearsome spears. That much I noticed, but Mrs Rutherford focused on the obscure detail of the nose. 'I've seen a lot of triangular snub noses on Yaka carvings, but how Senegal comes into it I don't know. Perhaps the Yaka once migrated that way and left their traces with Senegalese tribes before returning to the Congo. Who knows? That's the mystery of Africa.' She grew pale as if stilled by some reminiscence of the past, before being reawakened by the weight of the pots in her hands. 'This other one is more like a bowl,' she resumed, handing it to me; 'it has all the marks of the Pende style.' It was shaped as a human face and she traced its features with a withered finger, pointing to the way its forehead bulged like the sides of an English pear, its half-closed eyes, its pointed chin and eyebrows that ran like ritual scars from ear to ear. 'The Yaka and Pende are matrilinear tribes. Everything originates from your mother. And yet they're still such a fierce people. Just look at the aggression in these carvings, I can't understand it!'

'I know nothing about art,' I said, when what I meant to say was that I knew nothing about Africa. She looked at me as I returned the carving, seeing a Negro, his large black hands carefully holding up a sacred bowl almost in an attitude of worship, as a servant to some tribal goddess would have done dark centuries ago. I was no African though, and my fetishes and talismans were spirit-levels, bulldozers, rivets. I was a black West-Indian of African ancestry, but I was an engineer, trained in the science and technology of Great Britain. As she took the bowl she could have seized upon the irony of our situation, but Mrs Rutherford was typically sincere and down-to-earth. She assumed no prior knowledge in me, no ancestral treasure buried for centuries in the darkness of my mind which would suddenly reveal itself in the presence of an ancient artefact. She was neither puzzled by, nor scornful of, my ignorance but was glad to explain things to me.

The fourth hour was spent in an unexpected tour of the other African objects in her house. Normally the fourth hour would see the winding-down of our conversation, Mrs Rutherford gathering in her harvest of information about the cliffs, Guyana, my family, my politics and dozens of other subjects, offering me a last glass of her home-made wine with a generosity that was more a thanksgiving, before retiring to bed. This time, however, our pleasant evening ritual was disrupted. Instead, I stood before three ancient masks that were nailed to various obscure corners of her house like gargoyles. They were from the Bambara and Dogon tribes. She described the continent with an almost instinctive feel for the place, drawing my attention to the subtleties of form that distinguished one tribe from the other. She ran her aged hand tenderly over the smooth and polished surface of the masks as if over the faces of children. Most of them terrified me. Braids of straw or raffia hung from their scalps, a wilderness of bush entwined with feathers, fibres, strips of rattan and the dried skin of animals. Their ugliness was increased considerably by their prominence on the whitewashed walls of this English cottage. As soon as you caught sight of it you thought you were in the presence of a venerable England. Its exterior was cloaked in crinkled elm, which gave it a natural dignity. The hallway opened up into a large drawing-room, and you were drawn immediately to the fireplace. At the sides of the fireplace curious English instruments stood on guard as though they were keepers of the ritual of lighting up the darkness and giving warmth and life to the human body. Each had a different function – one fed the coal or pieces of wood into the fire; another poked around, turning over the flames to create an even heat; another raked the embers at the close of day. Standing before the fireplace and looking into the room you saw shelves bearing porcelain ornaments and decorated plates; walls hung with black and white photographs of ancestry; and, everywhere, books. Books which when opened creaked at the spine and gave off a pleasurably damp smell and the fine dust of another age. Books with raised holes made by insects in their pages, resembling Braille, as if even the blind could have access to the knowledge contained therein. Books that bore curious inscriptions in faded ink, in handwriting shaped by quill or ancient nib. *Ex Libris Joseph Countryman Esq. Dominus Illuminatio Mea.* Others were more personal, making me feel intrusive and uncomfortable when I read them because I was from the future they could not envisage, a future which could well have brought terrors and disappointments to their evolving lives, a future which ruptured the innocence of the moment. *For Albert, on being sixteen. May God keep you steadfast in your studies and may you prosper in His Grace and Wisdom. Your Loving Father*; *Dearest Annie, each word in this book tells your life and mine. Love John.* How was the father to know that Albert would indeed go on to become Professor of Classics at Oxford, Jack the Ripper's pimp or a leader of the Cato Street Conspiracy? And Annie, Dearest Annie, with apple-juice breasts that men gurgled and choked on, marble thighs that made men slip and break their necks; Annie who may have married John, lived in a farmhouse and produced six healthy children (brown and speckled like farmhouse eggs) who worked on the land and cared for their parents in their old age; Annie who, burdened with John's molestations and fetishes, perhaps absconded with an early feminist and wrote treatises against Royalty, Episcopacy, the Judiciary and other phallocentric institutions. I held the book guiltily and excitedly, as though I were a peeping Tom spinning fantasies from the partially glimpsed fragments of Albert's and Annie's lives, creating their past and their future, until I awoke to the pathos of their death, the pathos of the leather-bound volume drained of original colour and badly chipped. I felt then that I *was* a West-Indian, someone born in a new age for a new world. I was unlike Albert and Annie, whose futures were cause for eagerness or dread, whose futures were bound to the past like pages in a book following each other in sequence and ending in the hard board of a coffin. As a West-Indian I had no cause to anticipate the future nor to fear death because I had cultivated no sense of the past. I was always present, always new. It was as if, instead of having to read the book page by page, I could, even with culturally blind eyes, look through the tunnels made by the termites which bored through the whole text, and beyond, through the board covers, even into the substance of the desk or shelf that held the book, always making space, clearing space. When I held Albert's and Annie's books I felt that as a West-Indian I had no need to be uncomfortable in this cottage, which stood in their own lifetime, which may even have belonged to them, but which survived them. I could read their books, which also survived them, without anxiety about the strangeness of the world drawn by their words. All this because I had no sense of the past, no sense of ruptured innocence.

It was this confidence that Mrs Rutherford was unconsciously depriving me of by her detailed exposition of the African masks. She was in the full flow of memory, each mask giving life to some scrap of past as if its magical powers survived both time and the demise of its own culture. 'Jack was fascinated by this kind,' she reminisced, pointing to what she identified as a Bambara face-mask, 'as soon as he spotted it he paid for it in full, not even bothering to haggle.' I watched it from afar, trying to disguise my sense of the hideousness of the thing. It looked vicious and dangerous, the antelope horns which protruded from it making it half-man, half-beast. 'The Bambara were such gentle people,' she continued in a distant voice as if remembering some ill trait in Jack. I nodded as if in agreement, glancing again at the mask for evidence of tenderness. My eyes paused at the tips of the antelope's horns. 'Chi wara gifted them the knowledge of agriculture. The antelope horns represent the spirit of Chi wara. But it was the idea of blood that got to Jack...' I looked at the mask knowingly. 'Do you understand anything much about circumcision rites?' she asked, catching me by surprise. It sounded such a gross enquiry coming from her aged mouth but it was asked in sincerity, as were all the questions put to me in the six months I boarded with her. 'You really think it's vile, don't you?' she said bluntly, looking hard at me. I dawdled before the mask but before I could summon a response she eased my discomfort. 'I think you could be right. It could appear to be vile when you look closely into it. That's why Jack went for it. And yet the Bambara are a lyrical tribe. I suppose it's because this one is for uncircumcised boys. During the threshing of the millet harvest, they dance in them and beat each others' feet with sticks to prove that by not crying out they are mature. A lot of the artefacts Jack collected were about circumcision. Look at that Dinka drum over there. The tribe would thump it for hours during the rituals. The rhythm of the drum masked out the heartbeat of the young boys and their screaming. But that's only one way of seeing things, because circumcision was a spiritual act. For the first time in your life you disappeared from your tribe, held in isolation whilst undergoing all manner of trials and absorbing obscure wisdom held only by select elders. Afterwards you were returned to the tribe. You went back a stranger, no longer able to talk the talk of uninitiated boys, to play hunting games with them as before, to ogle the breasts of women as they bathed. And they either shunned you or held you in nervous respect. Even your mother and father treated you differently. That must have been the real pain, not the piercing of the foreskin. Still, I must admit that I used to shudder when Jack would come home with armfuls of these masks. It was as if he was hooked on them… as if they were sex magazines or something. Often, to save cluttering up the house, I'd send him back straight to the market to get rid of them. He'd come home muttering at me for being puritanical but knowing that he was the one afraid of being truly adventurous. It was all talk with him, all promises…' She paused on the brink of intimate confession before deciding to withdraw. 'They are no more ugly than your machines, you know,' she said, addressing my ill-concealed disgust at the masks. 'Most of them are used in rituals of nature. They invoke the spirits to bring rain, fertility, a good harvest and protection from drought and diseases. The Africans use them to control nature as you use tractors and bulldozers. A Bambara tribesman seeing your screaming bulldozer on the beach for the first time would think it a monstrous and enraged crab. It would be hideous beyond his darkest nightmares and certainly rob him of his power to describe it to the rest of the tribe. He would be literally speechless.'

I fidgeted in my chair and coughed as if to clear my throat for a considered response. 'It's odd that these masks rob strangers of speech, because the African world was created by speech. The world began with an egg, and the egg only hatched birds and animals and humans when the god spoke. His Word gave birth and motion to every living thing, like our Christian god. When the missionaries came with the Bibles bearing strange words, they killed off the African god and reduced the Africans to a pathetic silence, by making them speak alien words.' She looked at me mischievously then moved on to the next exhibit. 'This is my favourite of the whole collection in this house,' she enthused. It was in the shape of a woman, round and smooth in form, the artist carving an image of gentleness out of a rough piece of wood. Even the protruding belly-button, which made other figures in the collection appear deformed and vulgar, was part of the gracefulness of the woman's body. There was no stiffness of flesh, no rapacity of mood, no brutal angles. 'Jack didn't like this one at all,' she said, sensing my ease before the carving.

'Oh, why is that?' I asked nonchalantly, disguising my curiosity as to why he should have failed to respond to its sensuousness. I was embarrassed that my reaction was being contrasted to his.

'The breasts,' she said, resting her hand boldly on them. 'He wanted women with a child's breasts, a child's lips, every part of the body underdeveloped, almost malnourished. I suppose that's why Africa was his destination. Isn't that odd?' A look of bewilderment crossed her face; for a few seconds she retreated inwardly, trying to understand some truth about him, before returning to my company. 'Never mind Jack, he's the past, you're here now and I'm glad!' she blurted out with genuine excitement. 'Don't get me wrong now, it's not your rent money I'm after! Jack left me enough to supplement my pension and stock up on the good things. Let's have a last one before bed, what do you say? A bit of brandy I think, to knock me out.' She made her way to the kitchen and came back with full glasses. 'It's not a lodger I'm looking for, it's a bit of excitement. For years these masks have kept me going because they're so odd, so different. They're like nothing I am, or any of us in this village. But after all this time I was getting used to them. Then you came along. Come on, don't be shy to drink up, we've only got six months before you disappear.' She gulped the brandy, looked up at me and smiled.

The tour ended, Mrs Rutherford eventually retired to bed, and I went for my customary walk along the cliffs with her dog Jack. 'It's a Jack Russell terrier, that's why I named it Jack,' she explained. It was perhaps the only direct lie she told me in our months of friendship, and even so I could not be sure. There must have been an association with her husband in the choice of the dog. It certainly liked blood, chasing after rabbits to rip at their throats. Jack ran ahead as I picked my way along the path. The wind was high, blowing me sideways in sudden gusts and threatening to wrest the torch from my hand. It was the most thrilling hour of the night, the path empty of walkers and the villagers gathered indoors. The plumes of smoke from chimneys were barely visible, rapidly absorbed into the deeper blackness of the night. I brushed through heather and gorse and reached the edge of the cliff, trying to catch sight of the sea, but it was drowned in darkness. It roared and groaned like an inhuman spirit awakened by brutal forces, and as I stood above it on a spike of rock it compelled me to look down, to seek it out. The wind nudged me closer to the edge, its agent and familiar, and for a moment I was seduced by the prospect of falling, the exhilaration of wanting to know what it was to die. What was enthralling was the space between wanting to know and the experience itself, which would instantly annihilate all knowledge. It was the space I had put between myself and the African masks as I stood slightly behind Mrs Rutherford listening to her explanations. I stood behind her to shield myself from being seduced by the power of their ugliness, their inhumaneness. The fact that this woman – so solid in her presence, so seemingly rational, well-mannered and English – was my guide offered me protection against them, even as her dog Jack now barked about my feet, protecting me from myself. Quickly I withdrew from the cliff's edge.

It was the first time in my life that I had shown fear of the sea. I had spent all my professional life working against the sea. It was an adversary that challenged me to conquer it, thus filling my head with the grandest of visions, the grandest of ambitions. In Guyana I had reclaimed land from it, but the achievement was short-lived, as it burst through the sluices I had plotted to control its levels. I redesigned and repositioned the sluices, pushing the sea away from the shore, but after allowing me space to savour my victory it flooded in again. For fifteen years I had done battle with the sea, but in all that time I was never afraid of it or possessed by a sense of its malice.

Each night, in the first weeks of coming to England, I had stood on the cliff's edge listening to the sea, the wind swiping at my face so that I could barely open my eyes. I would look up to a sky ragged with stars, feeling that I could, given time, calculate all the forces meeting against me. I was the measure of all their colossal energy. There was an intense pleasure in sensing my eventual power to address and harvest these forces, one-tongued creation that I was.

But the masks made me withdraw from the sea, made me withdraw into a silence and a past that I didn't want to know and had no sense of being ruptured from. Mrs Rutherford's talk of African sexual practices seemed to breach some revetment in my life, destroying my self-confidence. The ritual of circumcision suggested that my ancestors were sliced from their land, the tribal hood or protective mask ripped from their faces. It was a history that could never be erased, for although the ancestors were long dead, their experience was commemorated in timeless ritual or timeless mask, testifying from Africa or from the walls of an English cottage. But in Guyana itself, there was hardly a suggestion of their existence, much less commemoration of it. There was no burial grounds holding the bones of slaves, no old sugar mills where they worked, no letters or books that they left behind, no carvings. Only lists of names and ships in the capital's archive remained, badly kept and used only by a few scholars. All they had was a papery existence, rapidly fading as the tropical sun dried the ink from the print and the wind blew it away as dust. As the sun bleached the page of colour, even the meaning of their blackness was lost. Perhaps some of the songs we sang and stories we told originated from slaves, but they were ours now. They were ours, we shaped our mouths differently when we sang or told them. What happened long ago was not of my making and didn't make me. The Europeans who ruled them two hundred years ago were not the same who ruled me in my youth until the period of Independence in 1972. The new black government commis-

21

sioned an artist to sculpt a massive statue of Cuffy, one of the first slave leaders, and it was put up in the National Park. But few of us knew who Cuffy was, and the statue, in which Cuffy flexed his muscles and grunted rebellion, only served to arouse discomfort in adults and terror in children. Parents dragged their errant offspring to the statue, threatening to let loose the spirit of Cuffy on them, for his face was scarified to the point of ugliness. What did modern Guyana have to do with an obscure person from the eighteenth century whose life we only knew in fragments, from comments recorded in English journals? Better to forget the past which was so intangible, and get down to the business of making a new country for a new age. The land was obviously capable only of bearing new marks, for the traces that the slaves left on the plantations had soon been covered over by the new immigrant workers, the hundreds of thousands of Indians whom the British shipped over in the nineteenth century to cut cane. Whatever tools the slaves fashioned, toys they made for their children, or drums they beat at weddings and funerals, had rapidly rotted away in the tropical heat and damp. The Indians re-marked the land, in the new canals they dug to irrigate the fields, in the new clearings they made to grow rice, in the new shacks they inhabited at the edge of fields, and the new bamboo poles they planted to adorn with Hindu flags.

I was nearly sixteen when my country gained its independence. I was at the beginning of adult life. And over the next two decades, I spent my time in Guyana preparing for the future, which to me could only be in the sciences. The landscape demanded human ingenuity. Rivers separating one part of the country from the next needed to be bridged; tractors and harvesters were needed for the fields; buildings fleshed in steel and concrete had to be erected, durable enough to survive the tropical weather; telephone exchanges and radio communications had to be put in place. But above all the sea demanded the mastery of technology. It was the sea, constantly breaking through the coastal stone wall that the Dutch had constructed in the eighteenth century, that made me a civil engineer. Every cell in my brain was absorbed in addressing the sea, there was no space for the sorrow of ancestral memory. In the daytime I surveyed it with scientific instruments, and in the evenings, strolling on the beach, I watched it with my naked eyes. It frothed and babbled against the shingle heaped on the foreshore but however much it fetched towards me, threatening to drench me in contempt, there was no question of withdrawal to higher ground, or withdrawal into silence.

I studied books on its movements, I flew across it to the other Caribbean islands to attend conferences on its behaviour and to read learned papers. And in those years of combating the sea, I discovered a history older than the human story and older than the human speech which told that story in terms of racial struggles. What destruction could Europeans wreak on Africans or Africans on Asians compared to the sea's frenzy? And what peace could we forge compared to the sea's patience? For millions of years it had teased and tested the land, biding its time. It had rushed in suddenly, flooding half a continent, then millions of years later withdrawn. An alteration of planetary movement, which could take aeons, would see it gulping up the whole of humanity. How feeble were our strategies to colonise the land compared to the sea's ambition! I plotted my life in relation to the life of the sea. How to shackle it with modern tools was the challenge before me, how to enslave it to my will and make it work for me.

The recent past became redundant, not only in my mind, but in the ways the sea destroyed or mocked the records of human effort inscribed in the land. For six years I worked in an area of Demerara in a land-irrigation scheme. We dug canals and sluices and we built dams and gates. We moved thousands of tons of earth to further our plans. On the surface the land seemed primeval mud and swamp, and I felt thrilled as Chief Engineer to be working in virgin territory, on a new frontier. No sooner however had we dug twenty feet or so but one of the shovelmen discovered several glass bottles which I guessed to be Dutch bottles. This was all that remained of the Dutch effort, centuries before, to do exactly what I had embarked upon now. The sea had come in and washed away all their effort. They must have abandoned their project and gone somewhere else to settle. The sea had broken their ambition, but out of pure mischief left the glass bottles intact for us to discover. And, almost predictably, six years into my project of ceaseless labour and with a rising sense of achievement as each year passed, the sea struck. In an overnight storm it wiped out six years' work. But I would not allow myself to be broken. What I needed was greater skill, greater knowledge of the latest techniques and machinery. I flew immediately to London to see Professor Fenwick, the English Principal of the Guyana Technical College, which the government had set up after Independence. It was Professor Fenwick who had trained me, teaching me the secrets of the craft. I was his first graduate. Over the years he had kept in touch, diligently sending me journals or news-sheets on seminars and conferences taking place in Europe. Now I would seek his advice on further training in an English university.

It was Professor Fenwick who packed me off to Dunsmere almost as soon as I arrived in England. He was a consultant to a major project to save a village on the Hastings coast. They needed a young engineer, and he got them to agree to take me on. It would be good, he said, and would provide me with first-hand experience. Afterwards I could proceed to do research at his university.

'Do you think I'm up to it?' I asked hesitantly. 'I've not had too much success back home so far.'

'Of course you'll manage,' he said, sitting back solidly in his chair. Surrounded by books, half framed behind an oak desk, he looked as distinguished and reliable as I remembered him in Guyana. He had been the secure point in my life when everything else threatened to crumble around me. He had aged somewhat since I last saw him, but he was all the same anchored steadfastly in the knowledge of his craft, and the traces of grey in his hair only added to his appearance of mature confidence. 'I've phoned an acquaintance in Dunsmere, Mr Curtis. He recommends you board with Mrs Janet Rutherford, who lives close by and doesn't mind looking after strangers,' he said, giving me a piece of paper with a telephone number. 'Curtis and Mrs Rutherford were married once, I seem to recall, something like that. They're a curious and isolated lot down there – it's difficult for outsiders like me to know what relationships they have with each other. Perhaps when you speak to Mrs Rutherford it would be best not to mention Curtis's name, in case there's some trouble between them.'

I assured Professor Fenwick that I would be discreet and I thanked him for his kindness. Later that day, having spoken to Mrs Rutherford and agreed terms for temporary accommodation, I headed excitedly on the train towards the sea. It was the same sea that I had done battle with for years, but the English end of it. I could not wait to discover how the rogue and monster behaved itself on the English coast: whether it was more mannered and restrained, as I imagined the English to be, or whether it charged and brawled in our creole ways.

TWO

For as long as the English have kept written records, Hastings has figured as a victim of piracy and plunder by foreign barbarians. Over the centuries, wave upon wave of Norse, Dutch, Spanish and French raiders had beached their boats and unsheathed swords and axes. Battles raged for days, the sands sucked in pools of blood and fed them back into the sea. North Sea winds snatched the cries from the mouths of the mortally wounded, bearing them in a litter along the coast, so that the outlying villagers bolted their doors, hid their wives and daughters in cellars, held their breath. But these terrors were nothing compared to the havoc wrought by the sea. In December storms, it lashed the cliffs, loosening their segments, causing tons of rocks to plummet on to the beach and bury into deeper oblivion the remains of human savages. The exposed cliffs then revealed evidence of even more ancient struggles and conspiracies going right back to the Valanginian age. The cretaceous remains of reptile, fauna and marine life lay embedded in an archive of sandstone and clay; long sucked of flesh, only their outlines remained, signatures on a page immeasurably older than those in Mrs Rutherford's library yet persisting through time, refusing the efforts of the sea to bleach them completely. Their resilience, however minuscule, however traceable only by the trained eye and complex optical equipment, still aroused inspiration in me, making me hope for the endurance of the massive bunds and stanchions I planned to erect.

It was not only the scale of Professor Fenwick's plans but their historical depth which provoked awe. Up to now I had worked in a landscape that could scarcely be dated by the scraps of records held in Guyana's few libraries; apart from the few Dutch bottles or Amerindian flints revealed by our excavations, the land seemed absent of data. The tropical climate and its teeming insect life had devoured the flesh of the few human efforts made in that part of the world. The Dunsmere Project, however, was rich with historical markers. For the first time in my life I relished their existence, since there was nothing of my personal history in the history of Dunsmere, no evocations of past failures or broken intentions.

Professor Fenwick's schedule of works was prefaced by a narrative of the coastline. Weather records kept since the seventeenth century, and mappings of the coastline equally ancient, enabled the scientist to chronicle precisely the sea's impact. Between 1637 and 1842 for instance the sea had eaten eleven miles into the land, carving out new coves and bays; in the following hundred years, the pace of the assault increased, seventeen miles of coastline being lost and some fourteen villages. From 1852 to the present year, in just under 140 years, eighteen more miles were gobbled up. The area under threat lay between two major reverse faults. The rock was in itself weak and friable, consisting of obliquely bedded shales, sandstone, blue-grey clays and pale silts which contained ill-defined bands of sphaerosiderite and nodules of clay-ironstone. It had a tendency to flake when subjected to continual wetting because of tidal conditions or ground-water seepages. Gales and strong winds hastened its degradation. Professor Fenwick's engineering plans had a projected life of some sixty years, and he had calculated what the contour of the coastline would be in 2012, 2037 and 2050. Long after he was dead, the engineering would remain in place, protecting the children and grandchildren of Dunsmere village; by 2060, they would have absolutely no fear of the sea, for by then a new, stable bay would have been formed. The dates were seductive, for they marked the paths of my own future.

The scheme was as clean and elemental as the very forces ranged against him, and the sheer quantity of materials was stupendous. Never before in my career had I worked with such astronomic figures. The whole scheme would cost £19,000,000 (a sum equal to the total industrial revenue of my country). To protect the soft clay toe of the cliff along an area of a mere half-mile we would have to create a free-standing bund on the foreshore, comprising of about 130,000 tons of rocks. A sheet-steel-piled wall would be driven into the foreshore behind this barrier of rocks. Finally the area between the steel piles and the cliff would be filled with three and a half million cubic metres of spoil material (chalk and grit) from tunnel diggings around the country, or imported from Europe, at a gradient of 3:2, to provide a protective bank to the cliff face. Gambions packed with stones from the foreshore would give additional strength to the bank.

I pored over the details of Professor Fenwick's plans as the train sped me to Hastings, reworking his mathematics, scrutinising his graphs, all the time bracing myself for the coming task. Only mental preparations would be possible in England, not the rituals of rum drinking and debauchery that the project leaders in Guyana would perform prior to setting off for the loneliness of the bush. It was as if they had to cleanse their minds of all personal cares, obliterate the self through alcohol and strange flesh before they could summon up courage to face the sea. They buried themselves for a week in a Georgetown whorehouse, in a carnival of sex, then awoke shivering and new to the darkness of the morning. They collected their tools and set off for the river, leaving behind the warmth and safety of the city, its shops, hospitals, sea-walls and brothels. The river stretched back from the belly of the city, bearing us away into a jungle whose only human memory was footprints left by Amerindian tribes long since annihilated, or modernised and resettled in Georgetown; footprints baked hard by the sun and which when filled by rain water became a perilous sea-crossing for insects, drowning those without a flake of bark to cling to. We travelled six miles inland before the river looped back towards the coast, deposited us then resumed its trail into the country's unknown past. A day's travel by Landrover over bush and marshland brought us to the en-campment. The coolie gangs were already at work, digging trenches or building mud dams, using nothing but bare hands and shovels. The two bulldozers had seized up and it would take three days before our mechanic could repair them. It would be a six-month shift, living *en masse* in tents or rough cabins. There was no alcohol because of the dangers of the work and the need to maintain human discipline before bush and sea. There were no women. Most men pined for female company, and a large animal moving in the hazy distance would become a dream of an Amerindian woman naked except for tribal decorations around the waist. They relived the loneliness and lust of the Dutch engineers of earlier centuries. By the end of the shift they could kill for women, exactly as the Dutch had descended upon Amerindian villages, making carnage and carnival.

The sex didn't matter to me though. Perhaps I found satisfaction instead in the cruelty of the whole endeavour, the hundreds of bare-backed coolies moving earth whom I controlled with a pharaoh's authority. Their livelihoods and thus their lives were in my hands, and they worked according to the drawings I provided, the inflexible lines like poles in their ankles. But there was no intentional cruelty in the drawings, or at least no more than my battle with the sea demanded. Although their neatness on paper told nothing of the hurt of coolie feet working in mud, they were calculated to minimise effort. In addition, by protecting the land from the sea, I would be creating hundreds of acres of arable soil to help feed the children of these workers. The marks I made on paper were marks of nobility. I had to believe this, even when a bulldozer toppled on a bank of earth and crushed both legs of one of the coolies. He was nameless like the rest of them: there were too many of them to remember and in any case all their names seemed to shuffle into each other – Lall, Ramlall, Rooplall, Lallsingh, Mansingh, Ramsingh, Balramsingh, Ramjohn, Alijohn… The British had shipped them from India to the West Indies, high-caste and low, Hindu and Muslim, all lumped together in a brown porridge. The way their names mixed into each other seemed to reflect the nature of the crossing, the nature of the ships' holds. Even now they huddled together in their tents at nightfall and woke up in one heave come morning.

The nameless one had stood out though, which is perhaps why the accident happened to him alone. He differed from them because he was always roaring and cursing at the top of his voice, as if to rival the sea's. He had a way of moving words, making the most dour surface suddenly ripple with life. If he had kept to moving mud with the mechanical dullness of the rest of the gang he would not have swayed in the path of the bulldozer. The sea-wind bided its time then blew him towards the machine, robbing him of his rival breath.

'Papa, you like Brahmin self, how this place stuff with book!' he exclaimed, entering my tent unexpectedly and waking me from my absorption in a set of graphs. I looked up, momentarily discomposed by his presence before reasserting my authority.

'Who gave you permission to leave your work and come to my tent? You know you're not allowed to enter here without Mr Wally Pearce's permission.'

'Pearce is one mother-rass red-nigger, I come and go where I please.' The vulgar bluntness of his reply silenced me and he went on the offensive. 'All Pearce do is stretch out in the sun and pine for Georgetown pussy. The man can't run nothing around here, why don't you get yourself a proper foreman, someone with whip in he hand and fire in he eye like colonial days?'

'You know the rules. Everything has to be done by the book, otherwise the bush will take over all of us. If you want to see me, you go through Mr Wally Pearce first.' I turned my back on him and resumed inspection of the graphs. He didn't leave though. I could hear him shuffling around the tent, inspecting my possessions.

'Lord, look how much things you got here, is like Georgetown Public Library! I never know before black man who does read so much – you is true-true Pandit self. Only Brahmin people got so much book-learning.' He rifled among the manuals on the shelf, reading the titles aloud, like a child learning to spell. 'H-y-d – Hydra – Hydra – Hydra…' He scratched his head noisily to provoke my attention. 'Hydraulic Engi-neer-ing. Man, is what name so? How come people does write fat-fat book, and not one story in it you can read? The thing contain only lines and angles and a whole lot of crazy drawings.'

'What is it you want?' I asked, spinning around and glaring at him.

'Nothing. What you get that you can give me?' he replied, looking at me scornfully. 'I only come here to gaze awhile. Sun hot-hot outside'.

'If it's sickness leave you want, you have to clear that with Mr

Pearce.' I suspected he was like all the other coolies, always begging for leave to return to their villages. They seemed to have large families and there was always someone poorly at home or awaiting burial. They themselves fell ill regularly, the mosquitoes and meagre diet taking toll on their puny Indian bodies. Yet, compared to the few African labourers in the camp, the Indians were diligent and obedient workers. The Africans made up all manner of excuses to shirk. They were terrified of the bush and longed for the gaiety of the city. The coolie before me was right: Mr Pearce wanted nothing more than to collect his wages and head for a community of pleasure and security. The Africans had long since lost their ability to survive in a muddy environment. Upon Emancipation they headed as soon as they could for the towns, shaking the centuries-old plantation dirt from their feet. They had cleared enough bush, dug enough canals, planted and cut enough cane and perished in sufficient numbers from malnutrition, disease and whiplash to claim their entitlement to freedom. Let the coolies take over, let them live in straw and shit. The blacks happily abandoned the bush and the land to the frail bare-backed newcomers stepping off the boats from India.

'Sickness scunt,' he cursed and sucked his teeth, 'this here is one bruk-up land but I mean to survive. I ain't no dhall-and-rice, hand-to-mouth coolie. The sea can leggo one flood like piss on the land, but Massa, I swimming, I not going under. When last you hear me sick?' He positioned himself squarely before me so that I could scrutinise his physique. He was in truth larger than the other coolies, the muscularity of his arms resembling more the African body. His face was pitted and scarred and the growth of hair around his mouth added to his look of uncouthness. He had huge hands which were curled rhetorically into fists. It was as if he had groomed his body in wildness, wanting to prove that he could cuff any adversary in the face. He could cuff the white man who shipped his people over, and he could cuff the black man like myself who now gave him orders and supervised him. Never mind spades and bulldozers, he could, when infuriated by labour under a hot sun, cuff a crater in the land to serve as a pool into which they could all dip and cool off, all three hundred of his fellow-labourers, his people. For they were very much his people

– this was evident from his extravagant behaviour when working among them. He led them in a Hindu song, bellowing out of tune, and at a faster pace than the rest of them, so that he finished first. He paused for a few seconds, waiting for them to catch up, then started another. Dutifully they followed. I sat under a large umbrella at the entrance of my tent, distracted by their wailing. I wished they would stop, that I could concentrate on the calculations before me, yet glad that the singing had got them into a rhythm of work. When the water-can came around it was offered to his lips first and he drank his fill; no one dared to look at him enviously; no matter how parched they were, no one dared hustle the can from him.

'Is one kiss-me-arse land you got here and you can keep it,' he resumed. 'I thinking to myself to take a walk somewhere else and get work. All-you know book, but all-you not know one damn about how to work the land.' He grimaced and spat on the floor of the tent. 'Is the wrong spot to begin with. Five miles east, yes, but not here. Is only killing coolies you go achieve if you carry on.'

'You better mind your words and not go spreading discontent among my workers, otherwise you will be in trouble,' I said, assuming an ominous tone.

'"My workers",' he said, 'eh-eh, like you act white man or what? "My workers" indeed!' He looked down at me and smiled as if he suddenly decided I was too civilised to be provoked into retaliation. He dawdled, unsure of what more to say, then turned to go. Something by the exit caught his eye and he hesitated. 'Nice-nice girl,' he said, turning round and holding up the photograph to me, 'is wife or is sweet-woman?'

I rose automatically and snatched it from his hand. 'Get out,' I heard myself shouting, 'get out now.' I wiped his fingerprints from the glass and replaced the photograph on the shelf, face down, so that no one could gaze on it. I went out and hollered for Mr Pearce. By the time he arrived I had recomposed myself.

'Who is that Indian that just left my tent?'

'I didn't see anyone.'

'The Indian who makes the loudest noise – the leader, you know the one.' He looked puzzled. He obviously had no interest in his job, counting only the weeks to his leave period, for he seemed to know nothing of his workforce. 'The one with the scar over his left eye.'

'They're all scarred,' he replied, more confused than ever, 'there's not a coolie here without some mark on his body left by snake bite or accident at work or somebody. Back in the villages they get drunk, they curse each other's mother or wife and they reach for their cutlasses.'

I took him outside and pointed to the man. He had a group of coolies around him who were more agitated than usual. He was addressing them and they waved their shovels in the air occasionally. He shouted something and they dispersed, going back to digging the belly of a new canal.

'Oh him! I don't know his real name, but I call him Swami because in the daytime he's always stopping work to preach to the rest of them. They look up to him like a god. At nights they gather round the campfire to hear him reciting. Apparently he tells them the stories from their holy books, about old India before the white people got there and ferried them away in magical vessels called steamships, and all manner of other nonsense I should imagine. The shacks they live in are decorated with pictures of Indian idols, strange, pot-bellied, sword-wielding or flute-playing creatures. I don't inspect the shacks any more because whenever I peer too closely at the pictures the coolies glare at me as if ready to kill.'

'Is he a troublemaker?' I asked, secretly resenting his authority over the men, which threatened mine.

'I don't know. He speaks to them in Hindi or some other coolie tongue I can't understand. I didn't realise these coolies knew anything but broken English. They're so secretive, you can't trust them, you never know what they've got up their sleeves.'

'They've got nothing up their sleeves,' I replied angrily, 'they've got no shirts on. It's your job to know exactly what's going on. I want you to find out and report back to me fully before the end of the day.'

Mr Pearce left, puzzled by my sudden hostility. He returned an hour later, a look of smugness on his face. 'They think you're crazy to be digging canals in this area and they think you need a woman to bring you back to your senses, that's all I've been able to gather.'

'What do you mean that's all? What the hell is happening? Go fetch that coolie now!'

He swaggered in and loomed threateningly over me. 'What Massa want? Just ask and if I got, I go give it,' he said in a contemptuous tone.

'I want to know what disaffection you've been spreading among the workers. What's this about my plans being unworkable?'

'Is not your plans not working that worry the boys, is your cock. When last you see it, when last you take it out and feel it lying in your hand?' Seeing me twitch with anger and struggling to summon up words of rebuke, his mood changed to one of playful mockery. 'Is only joke, man, joke. Like book-learning choke up all the comedy in your head or what?' He waited until I had calmed down before continuing. 'You see, you live all by yourself, away from we, like if we is pariah or something. When night come we cook, we tell nancy-story and skylark and get silly and break into song, and one man start boasting how bigger he cock is than any mule, and he take it out and challenge the rest to measure up. Is only fun, man, otherwise we never want wake up to this blasted sun and latrine of a land. Whilst you – well, your lamp burning late into the night, your head bend over book and your eyes bulging like is pussy you studying, but it's not. The Indian people them don't trust you, half of them would desert tomorrow self.'

'I can't afford to be as jolly as the rest of you. I am responsible for the whole project and for the welfare of the whole encampment.'

'True,' he agreed, nodding sympathetically, sensing that the very fact that I had to explain my duties to a mere labourer like himself exposed a weakness in me, or at least a desire to compromise. 'You gotta understand that we don't trust all these books either. Book make it out that you know, and we stupid, which is what all them Brahmin people tell we. That's why they squat on we like carrion crow for so long, leaving no flesh on the bone, just because they can open book and read how this planet and that planet line up to make misfortune, so if we don't pay them to say holy words we done for.' He paused to let his bitterness subside. 'And then, you so young, who go trust you?' When I looked confused he explained, 'For we coolie people, is only old people wise. And look at you – a few hairs on your face, less than woman's pokey. And on top of all, look how you black! How black man go know how to organise canal? That is long-time secret, all-you people lose it last century.' This latter remark stung me and almost against my will I felt myself impelled to defend 'my' people. 'Don't make me out wrong now, sir,' he continued in a meek and disarming way, pre-empting any counter-attack on my part, 'I have respect for black people. Half my village is black people, and I drink and eat juta with them and go to wake and sing Christian hymn and bawl when is burial time. But black people wedding time best! Boy, I does challenge them to dance, and shake up me waist and ripple me buttocks more than any one of all-you tribe!' He did a quick roll of his body as if the memory of village life sent a quiver of pleasure through him. 'Dance, boy, dance, all-you African people can dance and beat drum, all-all night! When I wake up next morning I lying in a ditch in one pile of creole bodies. My hand throw over somebody waist and somebody leg throw over me. Is like one big bugger-battie!' He roared at the obscenity of the thought and jerked his groin in my direction. 'No sir, I is not one of those Indians who say black people is Rawan pickni – you know, that they black like Rawan who abduct and rape up Sita in the Holy Scriptures. Black people is we-self, but how they different is that they hignorant-hignorant of how to plant garden and grow crop and manage land. That, sir, is Indian business, absolute.' He grinned broadly, his teeth flashing at me. For the first time I noticed that three of his molars were solid-gold inserts. 'I work the land all me life, I'm not no thief-man,' he said, seeing me staring at his mouth. 'I accumulate and I carry my bounty with me: you never know when crisis demand cash from you. Every single one on the bottom row on the left got gold filling. I saving up hard for the other side jaw.' He pushed his head towards me and opened his mouth wide for me to admire his wealth. I was astonished at the row of gold nuggets embedded in the slime of his gums. 'Eldorado, eh?' he beamed.

'With all that fortune in your mouth you ought to keep it shut more often,' I said, partly in resentment, partly in admiration of his character. 'So you reckon you're golden in speech too? I hear reports that you are the leader of the tribe, a man of princely words and enchanting stories.'

'Come come chief, you playing sport with me. I is a humble backward coolie, you know that,' he said in a mock-ingratiating tone, 'I does only talk bruk-up English, I don't know vowel from tree-fowl. Is bushman I am, from since I was born.'

'So why do they listen so avidly to you? How come you exert such control over them?'

'Because I wander all over the place, from the coast to the interior. I criss-cross and sideways the country, up and down, in and out, by and by, hither and yonder. I cross trench, canal, swamp, river, savannah and mountains, high and low, to and fro like the crow does fly. In my journeys I eat snake, turtle, alligator eye, iguana tail; all manner of meat these gold teeth chew and ponder on. Indian people does only eat special diet – no cow, no pork, no low-caste or creole food – so that's why they see me as special. I eat my way to high status and I crown my glory with gold teeth.'

'Come on, you're being deceptive again! I know you've got guts but it can't be merely alien food that makes them respect you.'

'Well, yes, it's more… It's all the strangeness you meet on the byways and bush clearings. I must have run from or parleyed with all the spirits of this land…' A look of mystery crossed his face but I wasn't sure whether he was having me on or not. 'Let me see now,' he said, stretching out his fingers to count the spirits, 'Churile, Massacuraman, Dutchman, Moongazer, Ole Higue, Bakoo, Fairmaid, Sukhanti, Dai-Dai… how much that?'

'Nine.'

'Well it only got ten or so, so I ain't missed much.'

'You don't expect me to believe in your superstitious stories? Keep them for your low-caste illiterate folk.'

'Well sir, believe or not they are still waiting to trap you, drown you, gobble you, suck you, sex you, blind you, cripple you. That's why you will never build dam proper, because you are sophisticated city man. You moving bulldozer to gouge canal without respecting the spirit living there. If you dealing with water, is Fairmaid you got to pleasure. You got to leave out food and flower by the river outlet, otherwise is drown you drown rass. If you dealing with mountain, is Dai-Dai you watch out for, otherwise they eat you whole and not even spit out the bones for a decent Christian burial. If road you're building, Moongazer will let you live so long as you hold your tongue when it appear. Say nothing, hold hands and walk through its legs when it straddle the road or else you done for. That is knowledge Pandit-people and Negro folk don't have, and that's how I command these low-caste Indians. And that is how you are bound to folly and failure. I bet you the spirits will mash up your work one of these days: they just biding time to get bloodier and bloodier. I know what I know and I protected,' he concluded solemnly, looking hard at me as if to contain his regret at my fate.

Now, his limbs crushed by the bulldozer, he merely howled. The noise disturbed all of us, so that the camp was restless for days afterwards – apart from Pearce, who lazed in the same mood of prurient fantasies as before. The coolies tended Swami with the devotion of disciples, changing his bandages, pressing wet towels at his brow to ease the fever. Each night a small group stayed awake to keep company with his broken body, mindful of every shudder, consoling him as he cried. We could not move him to Georgetown for medical treatment – the lengthy journey over rough ground and river would have killed him. We sent for a doctor instead. A week passed, no one came, and Swami's cries became weaker and weaker.

I paced up and down in my tent, unable to concentrate or issue my normal commands to the workers. It was as if his deterioration was robbing me of my own strength. 'He's only a coolie, there's nothing special about him. Accidents will always happen in this kind of work,' I said in a tone of desperation to Pearce. These days I was glad to seek out his company, treating him more as an equal than a subordinate. I needed to share his apathy, to escape from the distress of Swami's condition, but especially from Swami's dismissal of my endeavours. Pearce couldn't care less whether he met with success or failure. He had no pride in his work, no sense of zeal about our efforts to keep the sea at bay. At least Swami knew the monumental nature of our project, even though he believed I would fail.

I walked along the mile or so of sea-dam we had completed, each step a measurement of my achievement, each step taking me out of earshot of his howling, contradicting his lack of faith in me. I had made a mark on the land, a permanent mark, for the sea would deposit silt on the side of the dam, making it more and more sturdy with the years. And yet I could not quite convince myself of this truth, so that when I reached the end and turned around, the dam stretched in front of me like a massive burial mound. The mangrove and courida vegetation that ran from the side of the dam to the sea's edge mocked me with its swampiness. Perhaps Swami was right, no amount of human ingenuity could hold back the deluge from the backlands or from the sea in front. My drawings had imposed impeccable order on this malarial landscape, envisioning it as a precise rectangle of dams, canals and sluices. Everything was calculated to impose a hydraulic logic on this stretch of coastland, feeding the clay soil with sufficient water to sustain rice-growing. We would make clean, wide geometric spaces with our chainsaws where before there was a profuse tangle of roots and vines. Swami seemed to know that the task was futile, that the drawings were as fantastical as the images in Pearce's brain.

'One straight clean-cut fuck is what Pearce planning, like how your bulldozer blade does slice a line in the land. All-you people is straight-line folk, all-you does live along ruler's edge. The white man who used to rule you so fulsomely left you with a plastic ruler to rule you. If I take the ruler away, what you will do? Without the edge, you'll wander off in the bush and get lost and howl like a pregnant mule and turn mad with fright of bush spirits.'

'So if you don't respect the straight line, how do you live?' I asked, containing my irritation at his insubordination.

'I tell you already, I does stray about in circles. I does curl and disappear like smoke ring and reappear somewhere else. I already done convolute and circumnavigate the world before I come to this spot.'

'Oh,' I said scornfully, 'so you've been abroad as well as all over Guyana?'

'If "abroad" is at the end of the ruler, where the straight line run out and only mystery left, then yes, I been abroad. That's the place where you suddenly find yourself keeping company with Churile and Dai-Dai and all them others.'

'There are no Guyanese spirits except what you invent in your head,' I said, dismissing him, 'nor do I believe in all those four-headed and four-handed Hindu gods you worship. They're a relic from the superstitious past, relevant to the cloud-cuckoo-land you call India.'

Now, surveying my unfinished sea-dam, I began to doubt everything that made me, all the learning I had absorbed from books in years of rapt concentration. I began to doubt my blackness, my ability to work the land as my forefathers had done. Perhaps the Indian was right, perhaps all I had were the trappings of white people's ideas, white people's science, and I knew nothing else, nothing of what he claimed to know through circuitous contact with the earth and intimacy with its ghosts.

When Swami died I expected the sea to flood into the land, washing away the side-line dams we were constructing, polluting the canals with salt and choking up our sluices with tons of mud and sand. But the sea was no more restless than usual, there was not even the odd excitable surge against the sea-dam to mark his exit. He was, in the end, a mere frail coolie. I had momentarily believed that there was something monumental about him, a presence as unmanageable as the sea before us and the bush behind. But the machine which he scorned had crushed him, and that was all he was in the end, just another coolie. His fellow-workers were gloomy, as if they had lost faith in their lives, but my self-confidence returned. As soon as he was safely buried, I pored over my graphs and books with even greater zeal, lifting up my head only occasionally to wonder what would become of his teeth, what new interloper or fortune hunter would be lucky enough to dig them up a century from now, holding them up to the sun and marvelling, as I had done with the Dutch bottles.

THREE

Why, Mrs Rutherford wanted to know, did I become an engineer? She rocked back on her chair, a glass of wine in her hand, and looked softly at me. The last of the afternoon sun helped disguise the loosening of skin around her cheeks, the way it gathered in a ruff at her chin and neck. Still, her eyes were alert, like a lover's, quick to sense any change in my mood or any attempt at dissimulation. Even in daylight, in spite of all the evidence of age – the plumpness of her waist and legs, the webbing of her hands, the mottled patches of coloration on her forearms like bruised fruit – there was a freshness in her eyes which made me uncomfortable. I glanced away, focusing on Jack biting into a rubber duck in the garden. It was a large window, spanning the width of the sitting-room, allowing a clear view of the whole garden and of the sea beyond. Normally I would have mumbled something suitably high-minded about the challenge of mastering the tides, or something practical about the need for land reclamation, but I was aware of the presence of the masks. They looked so full of spite, evoking vague stories of primitive violence. They forced me to connect the smudged photograph and Swami's death, and, before that, the rape of Amerindian women, malarial fever, the drowning of my Dutch predecessors and the wastage of slave bodies. These images which I had buried piecemeal in my mind surfaced in a ritual sequence of shame. The masks glared down at me like the floodlights which had once mocked me, before I attacked them with stones.

We were a few years from Independence from Britain and the Americans had decided to prepare us for it by making a playing pitch in the village. It was for learning the game of basketball and it could be used at nights when the men had come home from the fields. The Americans were donating floodlights, a generator to supply electricity and all the requisite equipment.

I squatted by the roadside in the company of other boys of my age, watching with fascination the way the bulldozer dug its steel teeth into the soil, scooped it up, reversed a hundred yards then deposited it into a trench. All day it scuttled forwards and backwards, swallowing and regurgitating dirt. It screamed and screamed, blue smoke puffing from a long pipe in front of the driver's cab. It made the greatest noise ever heard in the village. We were accustomed to calves hollering all day from the moment they dropped when we removed their mothers to a distant pen. Their mothers bawled in turn, chewing the rope that tied them to posts, straining to be reunited with their new-born. Through-out the calving season the village was in an uproar, but no sound was louder or more cruel than that made by the bulldozer. The cows would pause in exhaustion and there would be long moments of stillness but the machine screamed on as if nothing could becalm it. Again and again it banged its mouth to the ground, made a nuzzling movement, then ripped the vegetation in an upward snap, taking it to a distance as if to eat it in private. I had often watched my father milk the cows, pulling and pulling, the roughness of his fingers making me shudder. I had watched with equal revulsion the calves finishing off whatever milk was left in the teats. As soon as my father removed his portion in a set of buckets and opened the pen, they broke out, barely able to contain their greed. They pushed their heads into their mothers' bellies, butting and sucking impatiently. Once, when every hand and mouth had done with her, I went up to a cow and peeped at her teats, expecting to find them chewed and hanging by a thread of skin. But they seemed to be in one piece, a little froth leaking from them, that was all. The cow looked at me incuriously as I squatted to examine her rear, then ambled off, leaving me feeling foolish and puzzled.

Whatever pain I imagined it to be in was nothing compared to what the earth must have felt when the bulldozer bit into it. The other small boys were excited by the violence but I stared at the machine in a state of distress. Three days later, the earth rolled smooth and covered in tar, the machine withdrew to the city, leaving behind a perfect rectangle in the bush. Four poles stood imperiously at each corner of the rectangle. From each one hung a lamp, like a coconut. Leaning from the outskirts of the rectangle were real coconut trees. They looked so crooked beside the four upright posts and they seemed to threaten the pitch with their unruly growth. The whole village crowded around the basketball pitch to witness the first floodlit game. No one was sure of the rules so the men improvised, bouncing the ball this way and that, kicking it along the ground to each other or butting it as it rose to head height. Whenever it rolled out of play a dozen boys including myself rushed to retrieve it, fighting and kicking each other. The women clapped whenever one of their men managed to reach the other end and toss the ball into the air towards the net basket. In the first quarter-hour no one managed to get the ball into the net. It was built for Americans and towered in the air way beyond the reach of our men, especially the coolies, who were obviously much shorter than Americans. And the ball seemed large and heavy, too much so for their small Guyanese hands. Every few seconds it rolled out of play since none of them could quite manage to bounce it more than two or three times continuously.

It was Alfred who managed to score the first and only point, for which he was immortalised along the Berbice coast, so that years later whenever anything special was achieved, whether by man or beast, it was referred to affectionately as a 'Freddo'. 'That is one Freddo of a bull I got there,' you could hear one farmer boasting to another, 'it already breed-up ten heifer and season not even start yet'; or 'All day the hens a-lay egg as if a Freddo up their backside.' Freddo became the spirit that caused things to multiply. Freddo also cured illnesses when invoked in knowledgeable ways, so that in a distant village, three suspicious Indian men with plaited hair and long beards, their foreheads strangely smeared in dye, claimed to be specialists in Freddo magic. They built a mud hut to serve as a temple and placed on the altar a picture representing Freddo beside that of Lord Krishna and Marcus Garvey. Their Freddo was imaged like an Indian god, blue-skinned, with a snake wrapped around his body and clouds at his feet. It looked nothing like Alfred, who was the most down-to-earth man in our village. In fact Alfred spent most of his life in ditches or in any patch of ground he happened to fall upon once his legs seized up with rum. He had not the slightest hint of divinity in this state of alcoholic collapse. He lay there until ants stung him awake next morning or a flock of sheep ran over him on their way to the savannah.

'Eh, Alfred, is you boy?' the shepherd asked as the last animal stepped over the body, exposing the figure of a man attempting to rise to his feet.

'Yes, is me man, it must be me,' he answered, wiping away the sleep and sheep dung from his eyes and peering ahead to identify the questioner; 'man, I need a drink bad, you got any rum in your back pocket?' He coughed heavily and swallowed as if there was sufficient trace of alcohol in his phlegm not to be wasted by spitting it out. 'What all these sheep doing in this part of the country?' He looked around to locate the spot he had arisen from, then realised it was the path to the grazing land, at least half a mile from the rumshop. His hand reached automatically into his pocket and fumbled about but he had no money. He turned around and looked at the sheep running ahead as if wishing he could catch up with a young lamb, kill it and take the meat secretly to Booboo – who owned the rumshop – in exchange for a couple of bottles. His legs though could hardly move, much less outsprint a young animal.

After the ball fell through the net Alfred had no further need to beg or steal, which was what he had made a profession of since becoming addicted to rum some twenty years earlier. The villagers nicknamed him 'Roosevelt' and offered him free drinks whenever he came into their yard. Small boys who once pelted him with stones as he stumbled about the village road, just to hear him yelp and curse, now came up to him respectfully, asking him advice on the game. Although many points had been scored over the months it was Alfred's that was remembered by them. He himself could recall little of the incident. He had wandered drunkenly on to the pitch and got lost in the welter of bodies, jostled here and there until he grew dizzy. He sensed a space between the bodies and made for it, but his escape was blocked by a huge ball bouncing towards his face. He put his hand up instinctively and the ball wedged between them. He held it for a moment then threw it up into the air away from him so as to free himself of it. What happened afterwards was terrifying, at least to begin with. Instead of being able to bolt through the hole in the crowd and make his way back to the rumshop in peace and quiet, he found himself engulfed in a storm of roaring and whistling. Hands held him back, clapping him on the shoulders or cupping his face. They raised him high in the air in a way he never expected them to while he still had breath in him. One day they would put him in a box, gather it to their shoulders like a bundle of cane and take it to the burial ground. No matter how destitute or leprous he had become, it was a sacred custom that none of the villagers would break with. The women would bathe him, put new clothes on his body and rest him in a box that the men had spent all night making from a freshly felled tree. Bells would hang from its sides so that when it was carried through the village the tinkling both announced his death and celebrated his departure to another, better life. He knew that no matter how people scorned him now or shooed him away from their doors he would be made dignified in the end, the sole focus of their attention. He never expected though to be recognised when still alive, so that the terror of being hoisted in the air was soon transformed to one of perplexed pleasure, especially when someone shoved a full bottle of rum into his hand and urged him to drink. Curiously though he found he didn't want to put it to his mouth and guzzle it down. He wanted to be sober, to enjoy their acclaim and jubilation. The way they carried him aloft, whilst others reached out to touch him or fought for a chance to bear him on their shoulders, made him want to cry. The lights shone upon him, marking him out from the bodies beneath and from the darkness at the perimeters of the pitch.

From the moment they put him down Alfred became another man, so different from his previous condition that none of the villagers could understand the transfiguration, not even he. Instead of setting off for the rumshop, his feet took him decidedly homewards to the shack containing the only thing of value he possessed, an old Singer sewing machine. It had been given to him years earlier by a missionary's wife for whom he had done odd chores, like weeding the yard or setting upright the grave-stones flattened by cattle that wandered in to graze. He wanted rum but she gave him the machine instead, determined to make him industrious and responsible. He tried to sell it but nobody would offer him anything, being afraid that the English God would curse them if they did.

Each Sunday morning, in preparation for church-going, my mother sent me to Alfred's hut so that he could make a knot in my tie. She reckoned that, being a tailor, he would know how to do it. My father had found work at a bauxite mine hundreds of miles away and he was rarely home on a Sunday to help out. Alfred had set up in business, dusting down the Singer machine, oiling it and tightening loose screws. He went about the village seeking work, promising to repair torn bedsheets or clothing for next to nothing. He had decided to start in a small way, learn the craft of handling cloth before venturing into the making of shirts and trousers. Alfred wrapped the tie around my neck, looping it here and there, then, holding me at arm's length, inspected his handiwork. Not satisfied with the shape of the knot, he untied it and started all over again but each time it remained crooked.

'I going to be late for church Mr Alfred,' I gasped as he drew the knot too tightly around my neck, 'you can't just leave it like it is?'

He prodded his finger into the collar of my shirt, trying to smooth the crinkles caused by the tie. 'Is true, you shouldn't keep God waiting, boy, but God waiting so long for man to repent that he turn old and grow beard and crook-backed. When rain fall is God dribbling how he so sick with age, you know that boy?'

'No Mr Roosevelt,' I answered, wondering what 'repent' meant. It was a word that the preacherman was always using. 'Repent,' he bawled, 'for world-end drawing close, tighter than a miser's purse and all-you will burn in hell like fire does melt gold. Repent, Lord God sayeth, now-now!' Soon afterwards the collection plate was passed around and it was piled high with dollar notes. My mother gave me a five-cent piece to offer on my own, and I wondered as I dropped it into the plate whether it was sufficient to pay for the repentance God wanted from me or whether I could owe him until next Sunday, when my mother would perhaps give me a bigger coin. Some of the boys were more reckless than me, palming their coins, pretending to drop them into the plate then buying cakes and mauby afterwards in the village shop. They built up a big debt with God and I knew they'd be in trouble later on, especially when the world started to go up in flames as the preacherman promised. But they cared nothing for repentance, biting into their buns like the devil the preacherman warned would gobble up sinners when the time came.

'There's lots to know in this world boy, so much that your head can't grow big enough to hold in everything,' Alfred said, perfecting the knot and sending me on my way. 'You ever see mule-belly when it pregnant, how it swell-up and the skin stretch like it going to burst?'

'Yes, Mr Roosevelt,' I said.

'Well,' he said, 'is so huge your head have to become and even then you can't hold in everything you can know.'

Throughout the service I thought of Alfred's words, wondering how big God's head was. When the collection plate came round I caught sight of my head in the silver surface of its rim as I bent over to make my offering. It looked tiny, as tiny as the five-cent coin released from my hand. I was so stunned at my image that I held on to the plate and my mother had to wrest it from me and pass it along the bench. She looked at me suspiciously as if I had stolen from it, and as soon as we were outside the church she made me turn out my pockets.

'Yes boy, God got eye bigger than one thousand basket-ball put together,' he laughed when I put the question to him, 'in fact all the basket-ball in the world don't even measure up to the circumference of God's nostril.'

'How big?' I wanted to know.

He took me outside and pointed to the sky. 'So big,' he said.

Each Sunday after church I made my way to Alfred's hut eager to swell my head with all the things he knew. 'How come you know so much about God and your head barely bigger than me own?' I asked him.

He was struggling to thread a needle, his hand still trembling from the after-effects of rum even though he had given up drinking months before. 'Because boy I repent and clean-up me whole body and God come in me stomach and fill it up. The whole sky now inside me.' He licked the end of the thread, making a point, then tried the eye of the needle again. 'Come close, I go show you what I mean.' I approached and he put his mouth to my ear and burped. I withdrew instinctively, nauseated by the residual smell of rum in his breath. He leant back and rocked with laughter. 'Is God's wind that bloat up me belly and belch out. Nothing wrong with that. You do it let me see whether God's breath in you. Come now boy, why you hesitate? Is devil you protecting in your belly or what? When last you repent boy?'

'Last Sunday, Mr Roosevelt, I dropped the money in, just like the preacherman say.'

'Well do it, let me see.'

I breathed in deeply, puffed out my stomach and burped.

'Good,' he said, his eyes twinkling with approval, 'do some more to make sure the first one was not fluke.'

I burped again and again, six in a row, until I exhausted myself and had to sit down.

I found myself drawn to Alfred's tailor-shop even though it meant missing a cricket match with the boys or going out to kill birds with our slingshots. As soon as I walked in he raised his head from the machine and burped. I burped back. It was an odd way of greeting each other but it got rid of the need for polite preliminaries. I would sit quietly as he resumed sewing, waiting for him to tell me something important. I looked closely at him, pretending that my eye was as large and shiny as the collection plate, able to reflect every secret in his face – the patches of silver in his black hair like liquid seeping from his brain; the smooth-ness of his black skin, all the more strange seeing that he had bumped into so many fences, rocks and other obstacles in his years of drunkenness; his nose spreading in all directions like a fig, and just as fleshy; and most noticeable of all, his neck, short and thick, with a lump in his gullet as if he had swallowed an egg and it had got stuck. I imagined that it would eventually hatch and the bird would peck its way out, ripping apart his veins and making him choke on his own blood. Whenever he swallowed, the lump shifted about, threatening to hatch.

'*Après nous le déluge,*' he said suddenly, pushing aside the pillowcase he was making and turning to me; '*C'est magnifique, mais ce n'est pas la guerre.*' I nearly slipped off my stool in fright. He had obviously gone mad, what with his burping and weird talk of pregnant mules, God's nostrils and the rest. '*Le jeu ne vaut pas la chandelle*,' he continued, all the while focusing on me with fierce eyes. 'You know what that is, boy?'

'No Alfred, I mean Mr Roosevelt,' I stammered, holding on to the stool's edge more firmly than I had the collection plate.

'How many years you got?'

'I is eight sir, Mr Roosevelt.'

'Oh…' he said, screwing his mouth up and tutting in pity, 'you still small yet. You born in the 1950s so you still got the whole century to learn.'

'Yes sir,' I agreed, wondering what a century was. Only strange beings called Sir Frank Worrall and Everton Weeks could get centuries. They went from place to place inside the radio to get them – one village was called Lancashire, another Lords, another Australia.

'That, boy, is call French, is what they does talk abroad.' When I looked puzzled he explained that abroad was a place across the sea. 'If you take boat and sail three-four days, that is "going abroad", especially when you reach land. If you don't reach land, that is what is call "being at sea", then you in trouble!'

'What trouble, Mr Roosevelt?'

'You does eventually go mad because only salt water to drink, then you does curse God and fall overboard and fish gobble you up. The sea-bottom full of bones of people who was "being at sea".'

'And what does happen when you reach abroad?'

'Well I does dock my boat and find a bar. Then I does stroll among the people, listening to how they talk and gazing at all the buildings. That's why they call some places islands, because you spend the whole day just eyeing up everything. And you feel as if you – I – is at the centre, everything there just to give you pleasure. Even when you got no money in your pocket you does still feel rich walking about the streets, because everything brand new and strange and is like life start all over again. You does feel as if you got more than one life when you go abroad. Everything is possible and so you never poor. And they got so many different words for money that you does feel that money don't matter. Money is not a thing, is a word, and when you get fed-up with one word it got another word for it, depending on which place you in. Here we call it dollar, but abroad it call *franc* or *dinero* or dosh. It come in all different shape and colour, and you can change one for another so at the end of the day the money not real. Nothing straightforward abroad, all is twisting and turning till your head grow giddy.' He paused and stared at the piece of white cloth before him as if colouring it with all the incidents of his previous life. He resumed sewing but his mind was obviously elsewhere. His feet jerked at the pedal, snapping the thread. 'Martinique was the best,' he said, 'that's where I pick up three-year job as pan boiler. That's when you boil the molasses till the steam turn into rum and then harden to make sugar. I was playboy then, fresh blood in me veins and pocket fill with franc. After work, is town we head for, all bathe-up and powder-splashed in fancy shirt, and trawl the bars. Ten-twelve of we end up on beach. Pretty black girls rustling French in your ear that sound like no breeze on earth.' He looked at the cloth again and at the rough sewing which revealed an inability to control the machine. Lines of thread which were meant to be straight careered across the cloth as if possessed by malice. Work was slow coming in: the initial flush of pity by the villagers for Alfred's new-found industriousness gave way to an impatience with the crookedness of his work. 'I used to be brown sugar, crystal, the light flashing from me feet, but look at me now… look and tell me what you see boy.'

I glanced furtively around the hut, afraid to look too closely at anything. There was little to see anyway. Old newspapers were pasted over cracks in the wooden walls or folded into wads and stuffed into holes. There was only one shelf, bearing his tooth-brush, a comb, a brush for lathering his chin and a soap-dish. Torn, shabby clothing hung from nails in the wall. The only colour was from sunlight trapped by a dusty window-pane, forming veins and patches of blue and yellow like in the piece of stained-glass window that decorated the village church. A card-board picture of Jesus was nailed above the door but the sun had dried and faded it over the years. The corners curled up, loosening the picture from the nails. The shabbiness of the hut was matched by his own appearance. When I looked at him I was unsure of what had caused his condition but I knew that I must never become like him. Somehow he sensed my resolve and began to counsel me on my future.

'Never drink, never idle and never curse God – if anybody lives so, is rich-rich they grow. You want repair bedsheet all your life boy?'

'No, Mr Roosevelt.'

'Well I do you a deal. You like to deal, boy?'

I nodded, half excited and half afraid.

'The deal is this: I want you to go to the sea-wall every day for three days and watch hard and come back and tell me three odd things in detail. And when you tell me, I got special gift for you. That's a deal, you agree?'

Every afternoon around three o'clock I did as he said, squatting on the sea-dam, looking hard at the waves and at the skies above. The sun changed colour as the hours drew on, becoming red-eyed as if tired of watching over the land all day. Slowly it fell asleep, slipping off the edge of the sky towards the sea. I felt drowsy but kept awake to report back to Alfred any strange occurrences. The tide was coming in, splashing and frothing on the foreshore, but nothing else happened. For three days nothing happened, only the sun sinking in a swirl of colours and the waves rushing towards the sea-dam. None of the villagers were around and I felt small and lonely, perched on my rock like a seagull lost from the flock. I thought of all the people and noises across the sea that Alfred had told me about. He had described the tall buildings, a mile high in the sky, made of glass and concrete. Then there were factories full of people welding and hammering or tending huge machines that belched out oil and smoke. 'Real life is abroad and big-big stories,' he had said, 'not like we people minding cow and sheep. This place here is bush, just look around, is only bush your eye behold.' Now, perched on my rock, I wanted to fly off to seek out the lands he spoke of. There was truly nothing here, only sea and sky, a wild tract of earth and courida bush growing before a ragged shore.

When the three days were up I went to Alfred's hut to tell him that there had been nothing out of the ordinary to see. As soon as I approached I knew something was wrong. The door was closed and I could not hear the familiar clanking of the sewing machine made by a loose pedal hitting the floorboards. I pushed the door open to see him slumped over the machine. He raised his head, screwed up his eyes and, recognising me, opened his mouth and tried to burp. Nothing came, only an ugly gurgle from his throat. He turned away and spat but the saliva merely hung in a blob from his lips. He reached for a half-empty bottle of rum resting on the shelf and took a sip.

'Here boy, come here and have a drink.' He shoved a bottle at me. 'Come closer, come, come,' he beckoned as I refused to approach. 'Is Sunday yet? You bring your tie?'

'No, Mr Roosevelt,' I said, appalled and hurt by his drunkenness, 'is Thursday today. I come for the gift you promise.'

'Gift?' he asked, 'gift…?', scratching his head and looking at me through glazed eyes.

'Yes, for spotting three things on the seashore, Mr Alfred.'

'Yes, yes,' he said, suddenly remembering his deal, 'and what you witness?'

'I see… I see alligator come out from the water and chase an iguana,' I lied in a soft voice.

'Speak up, boy,' he urged.

'I say I see alligator chasing iguana up coconut tree, but a coconut fall on the alligator head as he looking up and break all he teeth,' I asserted loudly, waiting nervously for his reaction.

'Oh… I see…' He took a swig from the bottle. 'And what else?'

'I see six-seven shark in the water, then a bolt of lightning fall from the sky and kill them dead-dead.'

'Well, well, is long time since I hear something so strange. You doing good boy, you must have the clearest eyesight in the village. What else?'

'A cow stray on the beach and four crabs catch hold of he foot and bite. The cow bawl and try to run off but the tide come in and drown it.' For some inexplicable reason the lies flowed easily. I could have reeled off another half a dozen incidents without hesitation.

'All what you tell is top-class story, bigger than abroad-story, but you miss out one thing.'

'What, Mr Roosevelt?' I asked, anxious to receive my gift.

'God,' he said, lifting the bottle to his mouth then changing his mind, as if the utterance had given him reason to pause. 'You didn't see God, boy?' he asked, looking at me strangely, his voice verging on sadness. His mention of God made me uncomfortable in view of the lies I had just told. 'That's because your eyes wide open, you look too hard. Go back to the sea-wall and sit down and then come back and tell me. You got to close your eyes if you want to see God, like if you praying.' He closed his eyes, showing me what to do, but the darkness must have made him giddy, for he slipped off his chair, the bottle crashing to the floor. He opened his eyes instinctively and groped after it to prevent all the rum spilling out. He struggled to rise to his feet but collapsed as if the invisible beach crabs were pulling at his heels. I left the hut dejected by his drunkenness and not caring for the lies I had told, not feeling the need to repent any more. There was no God, only sea and bush and empty sky. The horribleness was not in the sharks or crabs or hungry alligator but in the emptiness of the sky, which the sea reflected. It spread from the shore to the horizon like a piece of cloth containing no pattern or picture, more crumpled and bare than the rags Alfred worked on his machine. Alfred was a worse lie than God, what with all his talk of abroad and how he would give up drinking for ever, making me believe in big things; things that sounded as real and strange as the French he spoke. He was nothing but a crook, as crooked as the knot he made in my tie and the pattern of threads on his cloth. He couldn't even stand upright and walk straight. The only straight line he ever achieved was when he threw the ball into the net. He flung it up, and down it came, but he was so drunk that he couldn't figure how it found the centre. For all he knew the ball could have zigzagged and circled the net before dropping in, like a humming-bird hovering at the lip of a hibiscus before darting inside.

I passed the basketball pitch on my way home. I stood in the middle of it and the four lamps glared down at me with their silver eyes. My feet automatically kicked the ground, loosening pieces of grit from the surface. I pelted some at one lamp but missed by quite a distance. It was too high up and to hit it would demand pinpoint precision, especially if I were to get to the bulb, which hid behind a grille. I tried again and again with no success. In the heat of frustration I gripped the pole on which the lamp was perched and tried to haul it out of the ground, but it was too solidly embedded in the earth for me to budge it. It rose in a straight line before me, like a royal palm, superior to my puny efforts to topple it. Nor could I scale it, the wood shaved smooth, with nowhere to grip. I merely slid down and bruised my legs. I prized some heavier stones from the mud surrounding the pitch and flung these at the same lamp. One hit the grille but was too large to pass through and break the bulb. I scouted around for some more stones, this time selecting them by weight and size. After a few minutes of constant pelting, my arm beginning to ache, sweat forming on my face, I heard a bulb explode as a stone smashed into it. It sounded like one of Alfred's more violent burps. I went to the next lamp and smashed its bulb. My aim became straighter and deadlier with each attempt. By the time the last bulb was destroyed I was beside myself with rage. I looked around for something else to smash up, but there was nothing.

My mother was scrubbing the floors when I reached home. She was always scrubbing the floors, starting at one end of the room and slowly making her way with brush and pail to the other. When she finished she rose to her feet and went to another room, dropped to her knees and started again. I rocked in the hammock, watching the curve of her back as she cleaned the house methodically and patiently.

'What you staring at? You got no shame letting your old mother work and you stretch out like sloth? And yet how you sweating as if idleness is hard work! Go clean up your room now.' I rose and headed for my room while she shouted after me, 'Thank God you is the only pickni I got, how you so messy. As to your father, I praying he don't come back in a hurry, the house nice and clean when he stay far away. The Lord curse me when he make me born with breasts!'

By the time I had returned to the hammock she had progressed to scouring pots in the kitchen. Her whole life, it seemed, was spent in the house doing plain things on a regular basis. She awoke early in the morning, bathed, put on her ordinary clothes, more a large overall than a dress, and began cooking. She peeled plantains to be fried, chopped up bora and carilla to be boiled, meat to be stewed. Sometimes she would vary the cooking, boiling the meat and stewing the vegetables instead. Occasionally new vegetables would be added to the pot, yams replacing plantains, eddoes replacing yams, but it was the same task of peeling, stirring and providing. After breakfast she washed up, put away the pots, plates and cutlery, swept the house, laboured over the laundry tub until lunchtime when all the pots came out again with the plates and spoons, meat and vegetables. The hours before our evening meal were spent in sewing, dusting and conversations with neighbours who came to visit or to borrow small items like a box of matches or a spoon. She rarely fussed beyond the normal reproaches to me for laziness or untidiness, and never boasted. She seemed to have nothing grand about her, except on Sunday when she changed her whole appearance for church-going, becoming as beautiful and young as the painting of angels decorating the altar. She got up earlier than usual, washed thoroughly and spent a whole hour before the mirror, putting on earrings, hat and a long black dress with a large bow at the back and pleats everywhere, which made her look rich and special. I felt proud to be walking beside her, and when news came from my father that he was not coming home because he was living with another woman, I was not bothered, even though she broke down and wept. It was a ten-minute journey to church and I held her hand, secretly letting one of my fingers feel the softness of her palm and trace its creases whenever she was distracted by conversations with other worshippers on the road. I lagged behind at brief intervals so as to admire the way she carried herself. During the lengthy prayers I passed the time secretly sniffing the perfume she was wearing and sniffing others around us, so as to be able to distinguish her even in the dark with my eyes closed. Or else I would peep at her mouth as it uttered a prayer, noticing only the way it was moist with lipstick.

'I suppose you shirk schoolbook and go play basketball to-night,' she said, looking up from the pots and catching me staring at her. My tongue seized up with guilt. 'What wrong with you?' she asked, seeing the panic on my face. 'Don't tell me teacher Leroy whip you again today for causing havoc in class?'

'No, Ma,' I said, shifting uneasily in the hammock, my bottom suddenly awakened by the memory of Mr Leroy's wrath, 'basket-ball done, no more play night-time, Jamal break the lights.'

'Jamal do what?' She put down the brush calmly and approached the hammock in the same composed way that Mr Leroy would come up to me as I bent my head over the slate and scribbled away furiously, pretending not to notice him. 'Jamal what? What you say Jamal do?'

'He break all the lights with stones. I see him this afternoon, he take up stones and he do it.'

A mob of villagers headed by Mr Leroy set off to find Jamal. They caught up with him in the backdam, playing in the mud with other boys.

'Jamal,' Mr Leroy bawled, pointing to him with his cane, 'come here. Put down whatever you got in your hand and come here now-now!'

Jamal continued poking in the mud with his stick for a moment or two before putting it down and approached boldly. He confronted the crowd of angry villagers without flinching, whilst I hid behind my mother's body, not wanting him to see me. It was always so with him, the way he squared his shoulders and puffed out his chest at Mr Leroy, trying to make his coolie body appear bigger. In truth he was no more than a morsel of flesh, smaller than most of the other Indian boys, never mind the rest of us. And yet he was the most courageous, facing up to Mr Leroy, who was a huge Negro with hands broader than a water-lily leaf but heavier. Jamal suffered at those hands but said nothing, not even when the slaps shook his little body or the cane snapped in two over his back. Worse still was the fact that he was innocent of all misdemeanours. Whenever a ball broke a window or someone scrawled *Mrs Harvie does wear green panty*, *I pull it down one day and feel* on the toilet wall, it was Jamal who volunteered to take the blame. 'How can you write such nastiness about Mrs Harvie? What horrors pile up in that small head of yours?' Mr Leroy asked, tugging at Jamal's collar and poking his fat gnarled finger in his cheek. Jamal looked into Mr Leroy's eyes, and his calmness served only to incite further attacks on his body. We admired him tremendously though we were perplexed by his behaviour and by his capacity to take punishment. As soon as the class was over, the real culprit would go up to him guiltily, offering him a penny or a piece of fudge, but Jamal refused. His manly attitude made us treat him with special regard. After school hours we tried to compensate him for the blows he took on our behalf in the classroom. When we played cricket for instance he was put in to bat first and though he flashed clumsily and the ball hit the wicket we would pretend it was a no-ball and give him another chance. When his bat accidentally happened to connect with the ball and he scooted off but was run out, we would pretend he had reached the crease safely. He was the first to taste the ripest mango raided from a neighbour's yard, the first to pelt a stone at the turtle that lived in one of the ponds in the hope of smashing its head, the first to stretch his slingshot against the kiskidee whistling happily and unawares at the topmost branch of a tree.

To begin with, Jamal faced Mr Leroy almost in an attitude of boredom, though he must have been inwardly troubled by the presence of the other villagers. When Mr Leroy, barely able to contain himself, spat the accusation at him, raising his stick at the same time, Jamal only smirked at him. Mr Leroy brought the stick down, catching him on his shoulder, then raised it again as if it were a cutlass and Jamal a piece of cane to be harvested. A wail broke out in the crowd, taking Mr Leroy by surprise so that he hesitated, altered his aim and missed the target. The stick dropped from his grasp. A woman flung herself at his feet, grasping them so tightly that he struggled to retain his balance.

'Ow, beta, ow, ow,' she moaned, 'leave a pickni alone, no beatam, no beatam so hard.'

He pushed her away, kicking loose from her grip, and she fell in the mud. When Jamal saw his mother sliding about, trying to rise to her feet, his whole appearance changed. He still stood rooted in one spot confronting Mr Leroy, but now he began to quiver, the mask of resilience slipping from his face. I held my mother's hand tightly, not daring to look as tears burst from his eyes. He cried uncontrollably, the hurt of all the beatings which he had dammed up within himself suddenly breaching his small body. Even Mr Leroy was stunned, holding out his hands automatically to comfort him and to catch him as his body sagged and collapsed.

We renamed him 'Fourlights' in recognition of his deed in breaking the four bulbs, but he didn't relish the new title as he had done the previous ones – Cowdung, when he was supposed to have smeared it over Mr Leroy's bicycle seat; Phantom, when coins or pencils kept disappearing mysteriously from other children's schoolbags; Pokefinger, when Chandra, the most desirable girl in our class, with pretty curly hair and lumps pressing through her blouse, alleged that someone had crept up behind her, covered her eyes with one hand and slid the other under her skirt, hence the faint trickle of blood down her thighs. 'Shut your mouth,' he rebuked one boy who addressed him as Fourlights, 'I didn't break no lamp,' for the first time denying the crime and the heroic status it carried. He became instead an informer and Mr Leroy's most faithful pupil. Mr Leroy moved him to the front of the class under his direct gaze and began to pay special regard to his schoolwork. When we assembled to get the sums on our slates marked, Jamal was always put first in the queue. Mr Leroy deliberated over his work while we fidgeted behind, partly from the morning mosquitoes biting our legs but mostly from the stern aspect of his face. He put large stars against the sums Jamal calculated correctly, and when any were wrong he didn't tap him roughly behind the head as he did the rest of us. He smiled encouragingly at the boy and sent him away to make changes. When Mr Leroy asked a question about the spelling of a word and several hands shot up and agitated for attention, it was Jamal who was first called upon to answer. Formerly the biggest dunce in our class, Jamal over the months surpassed most of us in knowledge. He was the first to master multiplication of double figures and the first to read the time. 'This boy will become an engineer when he grows up. He'll learn to repair things, not break them,' Mr Leroy announced to the rest of us by way of rebuke for our incompetence. 'Who can tell me what an engineer is?' The silence in which we pondered the question soon turned into nervousness as Mr Leroy glared down at us. I wished I could lob a stone into his eye and finish him off. The class began to fidget. 'Who can tell me what an engineer is?' Mr Leroy repeated, his face turning sinister and impatient.

I decided to be selfless, to suffer on our behalf as Jamal had done in previous days. I raised my hand boldly. 'A man who does repair engine, sir.'

'No, boy, an engineer is not "a man who does repair engine". He doesn't do what you say he does do.' I yielded immediately. I had played my part, now let someone else throw the next stone. No one knew what an engineer was, so Mr Leroy was obliged to tell us. 'An engineer is a man who builds a bridge over a dangerous stretch of water. An engineer is a man who builds a dam against the wild sea. An engineer makes things spick and span, he straightens out whatever is lopsided. Now tell me again, what is an engineer?' He pointed to me and I stood up.

'An engineer is a man what does clear up untidy things.'

He looked at me as if he wanted to break my bones and then set them straight to prove his definition of engineering. 'You will never be an engineer, boy, do you know why?'

'No sir,' I answered, fearful of the consequences of my failure.

'Because an engineer is a man of grammar whereas you speak waywardly like the nigger you are!' A wave of giggles arose as my classmates took delight in the insult, but Mr Leroy silenced them by raising his forefinger. He stretched it out imperiously, held it taut for a full minute before curling it to beckon Jamal forward. He stood Jamal before us and taking hold of his shoulder led him in our midst as if Jamal were a church collection plate. 'Jamal dresses like an engineer. Notice how his shirt is buttoned neatly and tucked into his pants. Notice how there are no creases in his clothes.' He held up Jamal's slate, which was black and rectangular like the basketball pitch. 'Notice how correctly ruled his slate is. Notice how he writes neatly upon the line, the words not veering upwards or dipping downwards. Tell them what you will become when you grow up, Jamal.'

'An engineer, sir,' Jamal answered automatically and confidently.

Mr Leroy's new pride in him inspired his effort to achieve and he in turn policed the class, reporting all our misdemeanours, even though we would beg him, for old times' sake, or for a handful of fudge, not to tell on us. The boys began to call him nasty names like Vulture, Hangman, or more inventive ones like A-snitch-in-time-saves-nine and other variations of proverbs Mr

Leroy made us learn by rote: The-early-turd-catches-the-worm, Pride-goeth-before-Jamal, and so on. He in turn ignored us or put on a brave face, especially when Mr Leroy was around to protect him.

After school, isolated from the power of the schoolmaster, and as he made his way home, the boys would pelt him with pebbles, hiding behind bushes so as not to be identified. He flinched as they flew about his head or hit him in the back of the neck, but he kept his dignity, refusing to cower before them or break into a run. The obstinacy he once displayed before Mr Leroy was now reserved for us. There was no crack in his armour, it seemed, for we tried everything, from five of us 'accidentally' collapsing in a heap over him as we ran to field a ball, to secretly putting a half-dazed wasp down the back of his shirt when Mr Leroy was turned to the blackboard (one of the boys had saved it up overnight in a matchbox for this special purpose) so that when he wriggled and tried to remove it the wasp stung him. To our utter disbelief he merely shuddered and ground his teeth to contain the pain. He mashed the wasp into the floor as if performing an act of unim-aginable cruelty, all the time looking at the boy who had commit-ted the deed. He waited patiently until Mr Leroy had stopped writing and turned to the class again before putting up his hand and reporting the boy. He knew that Mr Leroy's wrath was worse than a nest of the most maddened wasps.

He moved as a superior presence among us for weeks, until one day in a fit of vulgarity a boy cursed his mother, comparing her to a heifer that bulls regularly serviced and caused to bawl, to an underground pit in which snakes slid upon their own slime and to similar images inspired by village observations. Jamal gathered in his limbs as if touched by a sudden chill. His back curved like that of a cripple. He began to tremble. Tears formed in his eyes out of rage and shame and helplessness. From that moment on he was in our grip. A crowd felled him, pinned him to the playground and vied with each other to compose the most outrageous remark in his ear, whilst he butted and whined impotently, like a calf watching hands roughing its mother's teats and draining its milk. As he bent over his slate, the boy behind him would lean over and whisper some obscenity about his mother, reducing him to such a state of confusion that he got all his sums wrong. When Mr Leroy called upon him to recite from the blackboard he suddenly turned illiterate, stumbling and stammering. Mr Leroy's patience eventually wore thin and he began to tap Jamal on the head again, first gently, almost to encourage movement in his brain, then full, open-palmed thwacks as in the good old days. This time Jamal cried openly. It was not the pain of Mr Leroy's slaps that made him collapse inwardly. It was the betrayal of trust that hurt him, and he cried. He had grown to respect Mr Leroy, to trust him, even to like him. I too was distressed by Mr Leroy's reversion to brutality. It seemed to confirm my intuition that there was no truth to anything, and that if there was a god he had long abandoned our land and gone abroad or back to England. I suddenly knew that I too must voyage abroad as soon as I grew up and could fashion a boat, even though I was not wholly convinced that such a place existed.

Every afternoon after school we went to the pitch to play cricket. The grown-ups worked in the fields all day and now that the lights were broken all basketball games had ceased. It would take weeks, if ever, before replacements were brought in from the city, so we resumed our traditional cricket. Slowly the nets rotted in the rain and when the sun came out birds perched on their rims and dropped dung everywhere. The wooden faces of the goals cracked and bubbled and lost their paint. The iron posts flaked. We climbed and dangled dangerously from them so that they were soon bent, threatening to snap off where rust had weakened the metal. As to the surface of the pitch the villagers allowed it to deteriorate as soon as they lost interest in the game. They no longer cared when cattle trampled across it, leaving holes which the rain filled, loosening the grit further. The cattle frequently butted against the four poles as they made their way to the grazing ground, so that they began to lean in all directions, as untidily as the coconut trees. The heat expanded the cracks opened by hoofs and horns; weeds took root, spreading along the ground, threatening to convert the pitch back to bush, as my mother and the preacherman had prophesied. 'Ash to ash, dust to dust, man make of muck and return he must.' He stared down at us, relishing the shocked silence brought on by his utterance. He licked his thick lips, wiping away old sweat and wetting them for fresh biblical warnings. My mother said the same after I had reported the destruction of the lamps but in a more grounded way, applying God's word directly to the situation of the village. 'Why everything black people handle become ruination and ash?' she asked, looking directly at me as I swung in the hammock. 'Is like King Midas in reverse. What he touch turn gold but we convert things to bush and blackness like we own skin.'

'Is not we, is that coolie Jamal who destroy the lights,' I blurted out as she loomed over me, her eyes bulging with accusation.

'Is weed and wilderness grow in we heart, you can spray and hoe until Judgement Day but you can't uproot them. I curse God I born one of we people instead of British or American or foreign. Them foreign people bottle up the electricity in bulb for we, and look what happen: as soon as their back turn, we buss the bottle and electricity drip into the bush and soak into the mud.' She retreated to the kitchen, muttering to herself, and although the sun was still bright she lit an oil lamp as if to console herself, poked about in the stove and watched the flames leap as they fed on fresh wood.

'So why did you become an engineer?' Mrs Rutherford asked, her casual question possessing the force of a machine. I had gladly let my past revert to bush but now she made me see again the clearing upon which we played, and Jamal squatting neglected at its edge whilst we flashed bats or chased after balls. All afternoon he curled his body in submission and watched us; he wanted to be part of the game, to be one of our company, but we never invited him to participate. So he squatted there, a brown lump, like the basketball we had slashed, kicking around its punctured skin then finally abandoning it in a pool of mud by the side of the pitch. God's eyeball had shrunk. Coated in grime it had gone blind, as I was to forget Swami, Alfred, Jamal and Mr Leroy.

PART II

FOUR

'Jack hated this place, it was too peaceful for him so he headed off to the wilderness,' she said, snipping off the heads of dying roses with a particularly violent action of her scissors. 'There's more wilderness here than he knew though.' She tutted at the thought of his stupidity, continuing to savage the roses.

To begin with I didn't know what she meant, the garden which she tended every afternoon being the very picture of order. At the far end was a wall of trees – hawthorn, apple, turkey oak threaded with honeysuckle vines – which ended in a privet hedge dotted with the dark berries of bryony. In front of the privet was the sunken pond fringed with campanulas and irises. Everything she planted was engineered to present a gentle spectacle of shapes and colours. Even the weeds were part of her design. Her garden was the major portion of her life. The deeply scented shrubs which sucked in bees and butterflies or the vines threatening to spread and strangle all the trees were extensions of her own character.

I sat in the shade watching her move among flowers, the names of which I was just beginning to learn, snipping at a leaf here, rearranging the earth there, her hand agile and passionate despite its aged appearance. Once, as she stood under the laburnum tree, inspecting its trunk, a sudden wind ripped through the blossoms, showering her with yellow petals. She became frivolous and gay, for a few moments the garden made her playful again and I was seized with a love for her, as Jack must have felt in earlier years. It was not a physical desire, quite the opposite. She seemed painfully young, needing to be alerted to the ways men could touch and wither her. Perhaps he was compassionate, torn up with guilt whenever he undressed her. Perhaps Jack had to take her away from such an ordered garden to a different landscape, one of extremes of lushness and aridity, before he could make love to her freely. In the end he seemed to long for nothing but sin and cruelty, abandoning her for native flesh. He had no desire to know the Africans except sexually, whereas the longer she stayed there the more sensitive she grew to their habits, covering her head and ankles at times, learning to pound yams, to chew kola nuts and grow accustomed to the bitterness, to speak sufficiently in their languages. She taught English and basic mathematics in a ramshackle school packed with the infants of the village. She learnt all their names, and how to pronounce them properly, as well as she knew the names of English flowers. The parents grew fond of her, inviting her to visit their homes, presenting gifts of dyed cloth, beaded jewellery, scarves and decorated gourds. Above all she learnt the landscape, the seasons of dust and flood, the unchanging patterns of tropical flowering, when zinnia and canna lilies lay like platters of flesh in a hungry land.

'You only know a place when you can identify the flowers,' she said, clearing some bush on one of our walks to locate some dead teasels. I examined them, assuming a serious air so as not to disappoint her. She told me how in previous centuries dating back to the Romans, the spiky cones were used for teasing the nap on woollen cloth. Each plant she showed me on the way seemed rooted in English history, having a use relating to the landscape of sheep, cattle and horses, or evoking some episode in the life of the nation. Turning a sharp bend in the path we came suddenly on a patch of poppies which startled and excited me. She paused before them, a withdrawn look on her face. 'They remind me of all the things we promise each other and then neglect to do,' she said, quoting some familiar lines of poetry about the dead of Flanders. I was suddenly irritated by the mention of war, which was so irrelevant before the actual poppies. I wished she could see them for what they were, sizzling with life, defiant amongst the tall grasses which would smother them; not tired symbols of some monumental stupidity. A slight mistiness came to her eyes and I wondered whether she was thinking of Jack but masking her emotions by an appearance of patriotism. This subterfuge, I had come to believe, was an English trait. As I idled through Hastings, viewing plaques, statues and public inscriptions, I wondered whether the English fondness for recollection of past wars was not in fact a way of marking domestic crises which, overcome with the passage of years, had grown mellow and mildewed in the imagination. Mrs Rutherford herself was mostly anti-patriotic. She grew vengeful or gloomy when discussing English history, and I sensed Jack in every utterance. 'All this talk of law and order…' she muttered, switching off the television abruptly in the middle of news of a coup in Ghana, as if to listen more clearly to the angry noises in her head. (Jack, I had gathered from a loose comment, had set off for Africa ostensibly to set up an English language-school so as to bring the natives up to a level where they could eventually manage their own country.) 'It's only the money our lot are interested in, how much trade we stand to lose.'

The violence of her mood surprised me. My own presence served to loosen her emotions. She had endured nearly thirty years of solitude in this village when she returned from Africa in the 1960s, unable to communicate any of her experiences to her neighbours. They were too alien to be shared, and too private. Now she could grumble safely to herself, hinting at all kinds of deceits and buried hatreds, knowing that I would remain a confidential witness to her confessions, a mask on the wall with big impassive eyes and rigid countenance. So she continued to make slight, almost irrelevant, references to Jack, leaving me to piece the fragments together into a biography of my own imagining. In the months I stayed with her I became seduced and frustrated by his history. I would scrutinise every object in her house, wondering whether it used to belong to him, whether he bought it as a special gift for her (an anniversary perhaps, or a moment of romance, passing a shop and seeing something gleaming in the window), but there was no obvious evidence of his presence. She gave few clues and these were mostly in her talk of flowers. Once I remarked naïvely that the names of flowers seemed so essentially English in their evocation of the lyrical – Lady's bedstraw, Lady's tresses, Queen Anne's lace, Dame's violet.

'The true English nature,' she scolded me 'is quite contrary. You have a colonial's sense of this place, that's all.'

I was stung by her opinion and tried to explain that in my country there were thousands of plants without names because those few who had ventured into the jungle had only done piecemeal surveys of the flora and fauna. There were probably whole species which had never been seen by human eyes, never mind recorded and studied. Guyana belonged in every sense of the word to the New World. The land was largely absent of names and the history evoked by names.

'That may be so,' she responded drily, determined to bring me down to earth, 'but England is more than maidens dancing around maypoles, which is the kind of image we gave the Africans while our men were pilfering their treasury. When I taught the children I told them of devil's-bit scabious, you know, those wild mauve flowers we passed by Mr Curtis's garden.' The mention of Mr Curtis provoked me into alertness. I wanted to enquire into her relationship with him, but Professor Fenwick's warning not to pry too closely made me hold my tongue. In any case, she had hardly paused for breath, the memories of Africa being too urgent to allow for interruptions. 'To be sure, the children were terrified by the very name of the flower, especially when I told them how it was used in all kinds of bizarre rituals to prevent plague spreading over medieval England. But at least they got a proper sense of our country as being every bit as dark and diseased as we told them theirs was.' She chuckled as she remembered the mischievousness of her lessons. 'As to Dane's-Blood – well, that really got us all going! I made them cut up pieces of purply paper into shapes like Dane's-blood petals and stuff them into their shirts. Then they took up twigs for swords, one lot pretending to be Vikings, the other Angles, and they fought like devils. Whenever a boy was slain he had to open up his shirt and let all the petals flutter to the ground. The classroom was awash with blood before the end of the lesson!' I was taken aback by this aspect of her past and by her passionate recollection of it, even now, long after my initial view of her as an English pensioner in a calm setting of cottage and garden had been shattered. 'What's more,' she continued, relishing her effect on me, 'I tried to teach them that England was not a place so foreign that they could not get there, which is what all the administrators, army officers and other –' she strug-

gled to find the word, then her eyes alighted on a spray-can –
'bugs, yes, bugs sent out from England told them. You know what
I mean, you are the last person I should be telling all this to, all our
talk of being so superior that our country was inaccessible. On the
other hand theirs was totally open, their minds, their fields, their
women, and we walked in and took.' The outburst drained her of
breath, she paused and puffed, gathering her strength for another
assault. 'Of course I used flowers, not Karl Marx, to make the
point,' she said, her eyes twinkling with life. 'I drew for them the
Turk's cap, which once upon a time used to turn the woodland
around here into gay Islamic territory. The petals curl backwards
and fold into each other to form perfect turbans. You don't see
them much nowadays but the shapes are still there. Those
rosebuds over there – don't they remind you of Turkish domes?
There are echoes of sultans everywhere in England if you look
closely.' It was getting late and she was visibly exhausted by the
effort of remembering, the original rush of excitement giving way
to a sadness and loneliness. She went to the shed to put away the
tools in readiness for another day's combat, for, given her attitude
to gardening, the secateurs, trowels, spades, shears, trugs and
hoes were implements of warfare against the past, and against Jack
in particular. This was no sedate Englishwoman snipping at
hedges, making that polite and comforting sound which all over
the country signalled survival of a harsh winter, house, possessions and family solidly intact. On the few occasions I had to
travel to London I would see thousands of people black like
myself. They seemed to live mostly in boxes made of concrete or
brick, high up in the air, where the only evidence of nature was
pollen irritating their noses. I wondered how many of them
voyaged to England because of teachings like Mrs Rutherford's.
It was doubtful whether they could ever understand the mythic
power of the garden which had drawn them here, a garden they
could never possess, being holed up in poverty and city slums. As
to Alfred's talk of abroad, it was as unreal as the rows upon rows
of tower blocks flowering from asphalt and garbage.

'England depresses you, does it?' she enquired, sensing a desire
in me for silence when I returned from a visit to London. I had
gone to Professor Fenwick's office to query some of his engineer-

ing computations which seemed incorrect, especially his assessment of the tonnage of rocks needed to construct the sea-wall. He had to dismiss me after a mere half an hour because of unexpected visitors, so I had left without resolving my uncertainty.

'No, it's not depression as such...'

'What is it then?' she asked coaxingly, as if offering to protect me against the nature of England. 'I really want to know. Since coming back from Africa I've not had a single contact with anyone foreign, unless you count Christie. But then, he's so familiar in his Irishness that I don't feel I could learn anything from him.'

'What's an Irishman doing in a place like this?' I asked, partly resentful that there was another outsider in the village and yet curious about the possibility of linking up with him.

'No need to bother about Christie,' she reassured me, sensing my anxiety, 'he works on the beach so you'll meet him soon enough and see for yourself what a showman he is. He's such a cliché of an Irishman, but then every Irishman I know is like him. You've heard of self-made millionaires? Well, the Irish are the opposite: they are self-made stereotypes, peddling the same images of mirth and misfortune. They are the scrap merchants of their own history but they make a pittance out of it. No matter how much they recycle their stories, the English will not buy, being too hard-nosed and unromantic. I bet he'll spin you a tale of suffering and ceaseless labour. He's the most indolent man in the village, a regular layabout. The only part of his body that works overtime is his tongue, so don't be taken in by him.'

Her outburst was delivered with such authority that for a moment I wondered what it was about Christie that really irritated her, and why it was that she described him as such an unreliable witness. All the same, the digression helped me to crystallise in my own mind the reason for my recent unease. At first I had wanted to remain silent, to brood a bit more on my misgivings before banishing them from my thoughts and concentrating on the engineering work ahead. Now her dismissal of Christie made me want to explore them. I wanted to talk. I felt excitable, as if presented with a rare chance to discover what I had been habitually burying in my mind.

'It's this whole business of stories that's been worrying me,' I

said, realising that it was not Professor Fenwick's specific computations, but something more insubstantial that had set me on edge.
'It's all those thousands of people I passed in the taxi in London, and
the thousands of brick buildings joined seamlessly in which they
lived seamless lives. I stared at everything and everybody, wondering whether there was a meaning to them, whether their lives had
stories, whether I could connect with them.'

'That's a very odd thing to say.' She shook her head in gentle
reproach; the exact gesture she used to scold Jack for misbehaving
or barking needlessly. 'Of course they have stories. They're
people, not engineering spare parts. What makes you say something so odd?'

'It's just that they looked so regular... almost like me... but
different. I didn't feel as if I could know them.'

'Do you mean you were coloured and they were white?'

'No, nothing like that, not at all. Nothing to do with surfaces.
We were all grey together, all dull...'

'Well, what made you different then?'

'I don't know,' I floundered, staring out of the window and
wanting silence again, wanting to avoid her gaze and regretting
that I had ever looked out of the taxi.

'I suspect the trouble with you is that things have to make
obvious sense, and if they don't, you give up. It's your training as
an engineer – everything has to be straightforward: blocks of
stone fitting neatly beside each other, cogs grooving into other
cogs and all that.'

'What else is there?' I answered, knowing that there was
something else but wanting her to tell me.

'There's the sinuous, the curved, the circular, the zigzagged,
the unpredictable, the zany, the transcendental and the invisibly
buried. There are stories enough in the brick houses, crooked and
abrupt stories that contradict their seamless straight line. The
tower blocks are perfectly vertical to your engineering eyes, but
they're drunk and blurred with human stories. And I've already
told you the garden I plant is a wilderness. But you don't
understand. Tell me, how old are you?'

'Thirty-three, why?'

'How much sex have you had in all your years?'

'Sex? How do you mean how much? What's that got to do with it?' I mumbled, overcome with confusion, remembering Swami's accusation about my virginity. She looked at me sympathetically, like a wise parent who had just caught a child masturbating. I felt dirty in spite of my chastity.

'Perhaps you can't sense that people have stories and you can't connect with them, not because you're an engineer but because you're still a young man. When Jack went to Africa he felt the same about the natives as you do about Londoners, until he got his hands under their skirts that is. He had an uncomplicated view of the place, a bulldozer mentality. They were monstrously black, half naked and living in mud huts. The next stage from such thinking was that they ought to be somehow removed and the place given over to people like ourselves.'

'Why did he go to Africa then to set up a school?' I asked, relieved that her focus had switched from me to Jack.

'He went to Africa for the sex. He'd bulldoze them into submission with his superior money, superior skin colour, superior civilisation. There was one unequivocal straight line between his lust and the fulfilment of it.' She looked hard and accusingly at me in the way my mother used to, as if I should be learning from Jack's mistakes. 'Don't you want to do like Jack and put your hands under an Englishwoman's skirt?' she asked suddenly, her voice edged with mockery. She waited for a few seconds until she was certain that I would not respond, before continuing to tease: 'Perhaps you can do it without Jack's nasty motives. Just the sheer thrill of nerves as you slide your hand up her thighs, the whiteness of it, the strange hungry flesh, the down of fine blond hair. And don't do it mechanically, don't gouge her flesh as if you were digging one of your canals. Soft, surprisingly oblique touches, insinuating and playful. Isn't that the way to seek out England's story and make the connection you want?'

I looked away, faintly nauseated by the possibility of her embrace, the closing of her fulsome creased flesh around mine. At this late hour of the night she always appeared unkempt and superannuated. 'Didn't the Africans retaliate against Jack?' I asked, moving the conversation on to a political plane. 'Why didn't one of them simply kill him?'

'Because they are remarkably restrained. They are not savages. And because of me, I suppose. I was their schoolteacher, they loved me and they must have pitied me for having to share my bed with him.'

'So why didn't you get rid of him yourself?'

'Because I was no madonna either... you'll hear the gossip soon enough if you stay for long in the village.' A look of regret scarred her face, her talk gave way to a painful silence. 'They loved me in Africa,' she resumed, forcing a smile on her lips. 'I admit that I was like Jack at first, bewildered by the place, not thinking I could ever push through the beads that hung at the entrance of a hut, enter it and talk to whoever lived there. But I made an effort with time, and I got to know enough of their situation to feel at home, or at least be useful to their predicament. They had urges more basic than Jack's. Most of all they wanted food. They prayed or danced or sacrificed for maize. To be able to plan three meals ahead was a triumph, what with drought one year and the next year, then floods afterwards. They lived for their children, feeding them first and last, going without, even dying, to make sure the young continued. Jack understood their culture and went about giving the children Cadbury nuts-and-raisins bars. He soon built up a grateful following and he would do with the children as he liked.' She shuddered at the memory of his behaviour, looking compassionately at me as if I could be counted among those abused by white benevolence. 'That was the worst of it, the way we behaved as if we were natural heirs to the place, popping our guns at the animals and frightening the natives. It made me know for the first time what we really are, outside of England and the decencies of the garden, the farm and the cottages. Of course I made them fight back, if only with paper flowers. These masks that you abhor are my spiteful children. As soon as we returned I nailed them on the wall to remind myself in England of how exotic the Africans at first seemed, and how appalling their lives proved to be. They've cleared a space for my loneliness, because many a visitor to the house was too uncomfortable to come back once I put the masks up. Even Jack couldn't bear to have them in the house, though he was the one who got excited by them in Africa. He slapped me once when I refused to put them away in the attic.'

The confession of violence did not move me. It was as if I had been prepared for it ever since I walked into her house and spied the masks. I realised now that they were not her spiteful children as she claimed, but instead sad symbols of Jack's conquest, abuse and abandonment of her. She had discovered no bounty in Africa, only her own pitiable female condition. The masks were terrifying at first sight, as she was to the villagers on her return; but when you looked closely they were mere ghosts of a previous potency, relics of cultures which Jack and his like had sucked dry, drained of magic and vigour more effectively than any drought.

FIVE

I took Jack for his evening's outing along the cliffs, strangely relieved to be in the open, away from Mrs Rutherford, her cottage and garden which held so many memories of distress and hurt. Jack, like his predecessor, seemed equally anxious to escape. As soon as I untied the leash he sprinted away into the darkness, careless of the clumps of thorns into which he dived. I could hear something scream as he bit into it, a shrew perhaps or a mole. His appetite for outdoor violence was queer given his almost docile behaviour within the cottage. Mrs Rutherford kept him in the kitchen in a space between two cupboards. He lay upon a heap of blankets, chewing on an artificial bone. He moved to the other parts of the cottage only when she permitted it, then he followed her meekly, never moving more than a few feet from her. When he tried to put his paws on the sofa to get at the balls of wool she scolded him and he fell back obediently to the floor. He still wanted badly to chew the odd shoe or mat, even though repeated reproaches over the years had tempered his instincts. Mrs Rutherford controlled him not by ill-treatment but by showering him with affection, cuddling him and tickling his neck as they sat before the fire. He in turn was devoted to her, pricking up his ears and growling at any strange noise in the dead of night. He was totally protective of her, not just barking at postmen or milkmen coming to the door, but treating me suspiciously whenever I went to the kitchen to make coffee. He would get up from his blankets and follow me around the kitchen, from kettle to fridge, back to kettle, making sure I was up to no mischief. When Mrs Rutherford and I sat talking in the parlour he was restless, sitting at her feet and staring at me. He would growl softly whenever I gesticulated, thinking perhaps that I was about to attack her. I began to fancy that the dog's behaviour may have mirrored Jack's, that the latter may have been similarly jealous whenever his wife exchanged greetings with any of the male neighbours. Was it a jealousy that became so oppressive that he had to abandon her to commit the very sins he thought she was capable of? Or was it that he wanted her to be more flirtatious with the men of the village, more provocative of gossip, instead of the appearance she had presented, especially when she was in her garden, of gentleness and vulnerability? Did he marry her precisely because he sought the decency she represented, hoping that his own desire for perversions would be cured as a result? Was he as confused as the dog, grateful for her kindness, compliant within the household, protective of her virtue, yet wanting to break free and torture weaker creatures, lesser prey?

Such questions intrigued, even obsessed me during my stay with her, because I wanted to find out the true nature of England. My main source of knowledge about England hitherto was the example of Professor Fenwick. I owed my being to him. I had grown up with English story-books but even as a child I distrusted the brightly coloured pictures of the butcher, policeman, grocer, baker and other characters who gave such order to England. The drawings were too intense, I almost had to shade my eyes from their glare. They jarred with the stories they were meant to illustrate, of simple English people doing simple jobs which kept the peace and made everybody live happily ever after. When I grew up I wanted to believe that Professor Fenwick was the true Englishman. He spoke few words and his quiet and modest demeanour formed an impression on my mind of the English character. Ours was by contrast boastful and boisterous: politicians promising more than they could deliver; professionals displaying their status by driving extravagant cars and honking at every cycle or donkey-cart that got in their way; the common traders bawling their wares from street stalls and open markets or haggling for an advantageous sale. Every day without fail Professor Fenwick turned up to classes, patiently instructing us in the theory and practice of our science. There was rarely a word of reproach from his lips, even when presented with the most bungling or wrong-headed of our projects. In the evening he went home, preferring to go by foot. He would stop at the rumshop and order a beer to cool off from the afternoon sun which reddened his face. He drank by himself, not out of unfriendliness with the locals but because he needed solitude to gather his strength after a tiring day's work. A few polite words were exchanged with the barman when he left, a friendly nod here and there to people who bade him goodbye. He read when he reached his flat, newspapers posted to him from England, and cooked himself a modest meal. Four years he spent with us, living simply and unobtrusively, without the least engagement in scandal, in spite of the whores who appeared like fat brown cockroaches and swarmed about the neighbourhood as soon as darkness fell. He had chosen to live in the poorest quarter of the city.

Professor Fenwick's influence on me was total. Not only was I in awe of his learning but his modesty made me want to mimic his every gesture and mood. I learnt how to mumble, how to avoid gazing into people's eyes, how to rest my forehead in my hand in an attitude of studiousness. I tried to look plain and sober, shunning the latest teenage fashions like Beatle-length hair and flared trousers. I drank no more than one beer and smoked moderately. I used every spare moment in the library. I cultivated a numbness to physical desire, speaking courteously to the girls in my college, never dropping innuendo or letting my eyes rove over the curves of their blouses. Such modesty however only served to heighten their interest in me, disgusted as they were by the blunt and vulgar overtures of other male students, their creole ways of ogling and prodding.

None of the students could understand why Professor Fenwick behaved the way he did. We gathered in the canteen after classes to discuss our various projects but the conversation invariably turned to the professor. He became the subject of intense speculation. Why would a man of his undeniable talent and capacity for amassing reasonable wealth in England abandon such prospects to work in our obscure country? Why did he choose to cross the ocean to live out a hermit's existence? How could he manage on the pittance our government paid him? And, money apart, how could an alert and knowledgeable mind such as his survive in a society without books or the latest technological instruments of his craft? None of us had answers to these questions, and curiosity soon bred rumour, it being our national habit to invent out of absence. It was a practice learnt no doubt from slave days, when we possessed nothing and were nothing. Our rumours about Professor Fenwick were spiced with malice, another peculiar aspect of our creole character derived from the past when our only means of retaliation was to curse or cheat. Such crudity continued long after the conditions which created it had disappeared. Any free black individual who showed promise of acquiring status and possessions was viewed with suspicion by the others. They tried to rob him, to pull him down to their level, and when that failed they spun malicious stories about him to destroy his reputation. And yet, privately, they were proud of him, wanting him to succeed on behalf of all of them, in spite of all of them. The wicked rumours about Professor Fenwick were our curious way of confessing our affection for the man. Some said that he committed malpractice in England and had escaped the authorities by coming to Guyana, assuming the air of a saint when all the time he was nothing but a cheap crook, worse than our own black professionals. Others charged that he was not as bright as we took him to be, an ordinary engineer in his own country who by emigrating to ours could shine and make himself invaluable. Yet others gossiped that he was a homosexual, discovered and put to shame, having to flee to save face. This last piece of malice hurt me more than it did Professor Fenwick, who continued his routine of travelling from home to college and back again, blithely unaware of the enigma of his presence. I didn't want the distance I had put between myself and female company to be misinterpreted. The fact that I was his favourite student, once a source of pride, now became an embarrassment. Quickly I altered my ways, making more earnest conversations with the girls in my class, even inviting the odd one out for a restaurant meal. I was unable to follow up such initiatives by taking them afterwards to the secluded parts of the National Park. Their accomplished talk and sophisticated city manners made me feel clumsy. It had only been two years since I had left my mother's house in the countryside and I still felt attached to her and the peasant ways of our village. 'Your father was one good-for-nothing crab-louse,' she would curse whenever I lazed about the house, 'King David self didn't have such crooked lust and looseness in he soul! Go study book straight before I put you out of this house to cut cane or wander among sheep.' I went dutifully to the porch and applied myself to mathematics. I knew she harboured great ambitions for me. I would not turn out to be like him, a lecher and layabout, not if she had anything to do with it. She would haul me up by the scruff of the neck. She should have been similarly resolute with my father, controlling the hours he woke, the hours he slept, his day's work in between. But she trusted him, letting him drink rum with the village men, putting him to bed when he eventually stumbled home, wiping the spittle and dirt from his mouth, staying awake in case he vomited in his sleep. She should have taken up a stick and beaten him in his drunkenness, making him sleep in the cow-pen downstairs instead of lavishing care on him. She had learned her hard lesson though. I would be different, she would bury me in books until the day came when I raised my head from them qualified as a doctor or lawyer. She too would be able to raise her head high in the village, wearing a fine hat to church, so elaborate that it would distract attention from the sermon if needs be. The son would have redeemed the father and her own disgrace of being abandoned while still of child-bearing age.

I looked up from my book, hearing all her thoughts even though she kept them to herself, screwing up her mouth and sweeping furiously. I wished my father had stayed at home, then I would have been able to put down my book more often and go gallivanting in the bush with the boys, hunting labba or snaring birds. But resentment gave way to pity as I watched her on bended knees, either scrubbing floorboards at home or in resolute prayer at church. Church was her only comfort and she spent as much time dusting the pews, polishing the cross and candle-holders and weeding the yard as she spent cleaning our house. Each Sunday, after the preacherman had counted the day's takings, he came to our door to give her a proportion of it. She tidied the sitting-room and wiped and rewiped the dining-table a full hour before his arrival. A meal of fried plantains and roasted yams was put before him. She ran and fetched some butter when he asked for it. She sprinkled on some more salt when he remarked that the yams were somewhat bland to his taste. She sent me to the shop to buy a bottle of lemonade for him. 'And buy soda and bun for yourself,' she said in an unexpected gesture of extravagance. I sat in the shop sipping my drink, thankful to the preacherman for helping us out. When I returned home half an hour later he had gone and my mother was taking a bath, at an unusual hour I thought, since she normally waited until the end of the day before washing. To my surprise she didn't reproach me for returning too late to give the preacherman his lemonade. 'It can keep for next Sunday,' she said, combing her hair coquettishly before the mirror.

Apart from the church's charity all the money we had was from the sale of the cow. She grew adept at cooking rice, coconut and garden vegetables in multiple ways, making each meal look, if not taste, differently, with the odd boiled egg thrown in on special occasions. She would not let me give up school and find work as a cow-hand or carpenter. We lived poorly for all my years in the village until I passed my final examinations to take me to the city. When the results were announced and I hurried home to tell her I was met with more gifts than the preacherman had received from her in a year of Sundays. There was of pair of leather shoes, two white shirts, a shiny pen and a briefcase. I noticed that her gold wedding-ring was missing from her finger. In selling it to buy me what I needed for college she had finally abandoned my father.

It was this realisation that I was wedded to her ambitions that made me apply myself to my studies, avoiding the pleasures and distractions of the city. And when I met Annette I felt that my mother would not have minded if I spent some of the little money I had in taking her to the cinema or restaurant. She worked in the college canteen where I ate every lunchtime, watching her lay out food, clean pots and wipe surfaces. She went about her work quietly, exchanging a few words with students at the most. She seemed oblivious of the prettiness of her figure and of the chatter of the male students, who viewed her as a potential victim, though hardly a conquest, given her poverty, lack of education

80

and lowly status. I saw my mother in her, and it was probably a sense of protectiveness that made me seek her company.

'Have you been working long at the college?' I asked on our first outing, not knowing what better thing to say.

'No,' she said. The brevity of her reply left me unprepared for a follow-up question so I coughed instead and stared impassively at the sea before us. A few boys kicking a football on the beach allowed me to pretend to be interested in their game.

'Do you come from Georgetown originally?' I asked after a long pause.

'No,' she replied, her eyes looking at the ground shyly. A considerable silence followed. I remembered that I had a packet of gum in my pocket, took it out and offered her a stick, which she refused. I chewed away as a substitute for immediate conversation.

I waited beside her at the bus stop. There were only two of us and I was beginning to find the solitude uncomfortable. She stared into the distance trying to ignore me as far as possible. I took advantage of her distraction to look at her body in quick bursts of appreciation. Now that the apron was removed from her waist I noticed how large her breasts were. I liked the way she gathered and pinned her hair back, exposing the whole of her forehead and face. Her young, almost childlike face contradicted the fullness of her breasts, making me see for the first time the prospects for the kinds of exciting sex which I had overheard the male students plotting for her.

'Brap! Brap! Brap! Is bruk the bed when I come with that child-woman,' one of them shrieked to his friend, ringing his hands in a gesture of glee. 'Country girls like them bursting with juice, one nip on she skin and it flood in your mouth.' I moved to another table to distance myself from their cruel fantasies. The years of solitude with my mother had not prepared me for such uncouth maleness.

'This talk too hot for you or what?' one of them shouted across the table to me and the rest of the company laughed. 'Like you is girl-boy or something. How come you never curse or spill rum down your shirtfront?'

'I bet he does really juk Annette regularly,' another said, coming to my defence, 'is those secret quiet ones like him who is baddest in bed. They look honest but all the time their minds wandering into whorehouse and bacchanal.'

'You think so?' the first one counter-attacked, 'the way he does act and speak so soft I'm sure he's queer.'

'He looks in truth like a backstabber and bum bandit,' someone agreed. They all roared and a few peas were thrown in my direction. I shrugged off their taunts easily, more concerned for Annette's welfare. She was within earshot of their vulgar talk but she maintained her composure, wiping the table-top as if totally absorbed in its dirt.

I blanked out my cruelty to her by total immersion in engineering diagrams and calculations. I intended no cruelty when after weeks of secret meetings and hesitant conversations I persuaded her to visit my room. After some shy preliminary talk I drew her to me. The eagerness of my action disarmed her. She didn't resist as I pressed my mouth to hers and delved my hand under her blouse. She pulled away though when I caressed her stomach and reached for her thighs. I held her forcibly again and she surrendered for a while to my passion, letting me place my hand where I liked before pushing me off.

'I don't want to,' she said, her voice trembling. She moved away and sat in the chair, rearranging her clothing.

'Why not?' I asked impotently, unsure of how to proceed but knowing that I had to have sex with her, the brief feel of her flesh arousing an uncontrollable need.

'I just don't want to. I don't know why.' She curled up her body to make it smaller. For a moment I relented, out of pity for her helplessness, before being overcome again by the prospect of her naked breasts.

'You're always so unsure. I can never get more than two words out of your mouth at any one time,' I said, my tone of voice unexpectedly angry. She too was alarmed, staring at the floor as if she wished she had a mop in her hand for protection. 'How come you always act like a dumb servant girl?' I persisted in spite of myself, watching her quiver. '"Yes. No. Yes. Maybe. I don't know," that's all I ever get out of you. The only thing you seem to put your mind to is scrubbing. God knows why I bothered to go out with you for so long.' I suddenly remembered the expense of restaurant meals and cinema tickets, which at the time I could barely afford but which I paid no heed to in gestures of generosity. 'I've wasted my time with you haven't I?' She said nothing.

Afterwards I felt sorry for having bullied her into acquiescence. She had lain softly on the bed, hardly moving or responding as I took her in a fit of lust. The sight of her large naked breasts provoked a curious desire to hurt her. I gripped her cruelly to my body, forcing my might on her. I wanted to be satisfied and her limpness only made me more determined. It was only when the sense of pleasure drained from me and I lay on my back staring at the fan whipping through a cobwebbed ceiling that I thought of her distress. As soon as I had done with her she had turned away as if too ashamed to face me. Now it was I who was lost for words. 'I love you,' I lied.

So this was what my father must have wanted from his new woman, I thought to myself when she left, this convulsion of flesh, this crazed need for physical satisfaction whatever the human cost. I had not bothered to know Annette. I had merely spent weeks baiting her, my seeming generosity and care a means of making her trust me, become dependent on me. I was worse than the louts who lusted after her, more cunning and destructive. I had listened to the scraps that came from her mouth, brief intimations of her village childhood, the dreadful hand-to-mouth existence of her family, the rare chance that came her way to travel to the city and find work, but all the time I was calculating a mode of entry into her body. I listened only to be able to assess her weakness, to break her down to manageable parts like the equations I was learning by rote. Afterwards I embraced her, overcome by a sense not only of the wretchedness of my action but of the poverty she embodied, which was the poverty of a land of malarial bush and swamp; a poverty which bred human cruelty and was worsened by it. My father's desertion, Jamal's sobbing, Roosevelt's drunken lies, Mr Leroy's bullying... and now my own craftiness. I held her body urgently, wanting to be intimate, to be redemptive and for the first time kissed her lips tenderly. She remained limp in my arms.

It was an immense relief to resume classes and be in the company of Professor Fenwick, who seemed invulnerable to the uncouthness of our country. Speculations about his background continued to be rife and although I was drawn into the mystery of his past, wondering what cruelties in England he was fleeing from, I was comforted by his appearance of quiet efficiency and studiousness. More than ever I resolved to imitate him, especially his way of speaking softly as if he didn't want to be heard, as if words were to be used sparingly rather than for the purpose of self-promotion. I settled down to my scientific work determined to be self-effacing, frugal in speech, placing trust instead in the fluency of the numbers and graphs contained in my books. Never again would I fantasise and grunt as I had done with Annette, bruising my mouth and hers. In two months' time I would graduate and move away, leaving my shame and hers behind.

'You wasn't for me,' she said when the time came. We had resumed our friendship, though there was always nervousness and longer than usual periods of silence when we met at the sea-wall or in a restaurant. I was afraid that she may be pregnant. She shook her head when I asked. 'You did only pity me really, not love.'

'You were pretty and I was a rascal like the rest of them,' I confessed.

'I know, but you was different too.'

'How different?' I asked, grasping at a chance to redeem my character in my own eyes.

'I make for broomstick and duster and hurtful men like you.'

'So I am like all the rest,' I urged, wanting her to confirm that I was as heartless as my father.

'No, you was more confused that's all. The rest want to abuse me straight, but you only want to try it out. Afterwards you full of repentance.'

'Repentance?' I asked, startled by her mention of the word which had haunted my boyhood, 'how do you mean?' But she said nothing else, retreating into herself, into a space as cramped and suffocating as the village she had come from, a handful of homes in a pocket of bush on the banks of a river too dangerous to cross except by boats with engines. Its strong hidden currents frequently capsized the small canoes they paddled, sucking in a body and feeding it downstream to piranha. There seemed to be no way into the village and no way out except by hazarding one's life. Those born into the place were doomed to stay there, inheriting the wretched plots of clearing from their parents, existing on a diet of yams, plantains, wildfowl and fish. She had managed to get out, only to be trapped in a canteen in the service of male students who wanted to force her into the tighter space of their lust. And yet the word 'repentance' came from her mouth so naturally, Alfred's big word which had signified to me the whole broadness of the sky in which God lived. 'So big,' he had said, pointing to the sky before returning to the patch of cloth on his machine.

SIX

I stood with Mrs Rutherford on a raised mound of the cliffs and watched the sea reaching for the shore, recoiling, pressing forwards again, a constant anxiety, like a disturbed patient pacing his room, or fidgeting within a straight-jacket. Behind me, a green land dissected into fields of barley and wheat dipped suddenly into a valley then staggered up in a lopsided curve only to collapse further on. Cottages were sprinkled here and there, each seeded in its own private bed and curtained off by trees, the meagre remains of the woodland that once flourished for miles around. Axes, then chainsaws, had reduced the forest into arable plots and, while men were hacking the land behind, the sea was equally intent on the cliff before. Still there was a certain beauty in the sparseness of the landscape, a settled order such as follows inevitably from centuries of plunder. The generations contented themselves with the clearings they had made. To chop down more trees would be to lay waste to the soil and threaten to convert it into barren rock. So they settled down, multiplied and prospered within the boundaries they had marked in the land, marks enshrined in law, protecting neighbour from neighbour. Fields of barley and wheat, hedges that defined territory, a stabilised woodland, secluded cottages and a sense of the Law of the Land – this was Dunsmere. Nothing, it seemed, had happened to the village in living memory. Other places had apparently suffered from an influx of young city people. They disturbed the character of village life by their loudness and over-friendliness to the locals. They gave barmen and waitresses extravagant tips, as if to bribe their way into the community. Their large, expensive cars took over the whole of the village road, forcing the locals on to the muddy verges. Or else the council were moving in the lower orders, rows of brick boxes appearing on slopes once thick with beech. Dunsmere though was preserved from the world outside its boundaries; the perilous state of the cliff meant that no one wanted to invest in property. From afar it looked like waxwork, colourful and still. I pictured it as I had often gazed upon the brightly coloured drawings in my colonial story-book, holding it at arm's length to minimise the glare and gain a truer perspective; drawings of English Christmas scenes, villagers dressed in tweed and scarves, snow glistening like wax from roof-tops, candles of icicles hanging from eaves.

'Weeds, weeds, weeds,' Mrs Rutherford said with particular venom, pointing me to some more teasels as we continued our walk along the cliff-top. She stooped to examine some daisies. 'That's how they got the land. They wiped out the weaker folk, joining one stolen field to another, then built castles to defend their loot, and gave themselves grand titles like Baron or Duke. The history of England is a nasty business.' She looked at me sternly. 'It's the English sickness. We carried it all over the world. Boatload of ivory or boatload of black bodies, it was all the same. But then you would know that first-hand, coming from the colonies.' An old woman in rimless glasses and a faded straw hat approached us along the path. She walked slowly and carefully as if she was afraid of stumbling on a stone and not being able to get up, arthritis having locked her joints more rigidly than the claws of a dead crab.

'Good-morning Mrs Goldsmith, lovely day today.'

'A lovely day Mrs Rutherford,' the old lady replied, screwing up her eyes to get a better look at me through thick lenses. 'And how do you do, young sir?' Before I could answer she was on her way, anxious to reach her destination in one piece.

'And to think that such sturdy beggars as our ancestors produced such modern geriatrics,' Mrs Rutherford whispered to me as soon as the old lady passed. I stayed silent, refusing to be provoked. 'At least the woman has character,' she resumed in the same conspiratorial tone. 'Crooked from birth by all accounts. They say she was born feet-first, all squashed and leaking out her brains. She was stuck in there for hours, wilfully refusing to budge. It took two hefty midwives to yank her out. It was like a scene from an abattoir. Now that she's out she'll stay out – it'll be another thirty years before she dies and even then they'll have to nail her in. The rest come and go quietly, here for their allotted period, then expire into nowhere. Retired teachers, retired civil servants, retired farmers, retired army officers, mostly indoors, stirring in their gardens when the weather allows. Their children have long grown up and gone. Some of the villagers had big bureaucratic jobs in London, making decisions which determined the lives of people living beyond this country, people like yourself. Some may have started wars or famines with their paperwork for all we know. And yet they were all so calm, so withdrawn, keeping their crimes to themselves, their bodies scrubbed, not the slightest whiff of blood about them. Like your Londoners – unbroken on the surface, but dig the spade in and when you turn the dirt over they're crawling with fables. At least Mrs Goldsmith makes her mark and displays it. Her stick digs spiteful holes in the ground as she stumbles along. You can trace her underground journey from the tell-tale scoops of earth above, like a badger set.'

'They couldn't have been that drearily barbaric,' I protested, irritated by her excessive contempt for the villagers. True, I had hardly seen any of them since my arrival, so could only confirm what she said of their infirmity. The ones I passed on my walks were all elderly. They were accompanied by dogs which so absorbed their attention that they seemed barely to notice me. They mumbled greetings and moved on, but I took no offence since I myself was unsure of how to acknowledge them.

'Oh, there were – and still are – outbreaks of colourful community,' she conceded, 'hearty salutations at Christmas, bell-ringing, that kind of thing. Or when someone fell seriously ill the cards would pour in, neighbours rally around with pots of tea and consoling words. It's English kindness, but I wonder whether it's any more than the spirit in the exclusive clubs we set up in Calcutta or Lagos. Being English is like having a virus which we pass among ourselves and become immune to. We're bound together by a shared and neutralised virus which suddenly flares into dreadful life among alien peoples who come into contact with us.' The bitterness of her tone made conversation impossible. We walked on in silence. I could sense her frustration with me. She wanted me to sympathise with her hatred, but the memory of Professor Fenwick's kindness contradicted her image of her own people.

'I suppose I go over the top sometimes,' she conceded after an embarrassed pause. 'Jack used to say that about me. "Calm down Janet," he'd say in that maddeningly gentle voice of his, as if coaxing an obstinate child.' She picked a daisy and held it up to the sun as if examining it for blight. 'I wasn't always like this you know. When Jack brought me to Dunsmere I was so glad to be with him in a new place and in our own house. He had inherited a small farm and worked hard to breed poultry. I loved helping him out. The first few months were happy, there was so much to do on the farm and in the house, not a spare moment to brood or worry. We were married for a year or so and I badly wanted to be a proper wife, even when things were cooling between us…' She twirled the flower by its stem in a nervous action then let it drop to the ground. She stared at it as if deciding whether to pick it up or let it lie. 'I even made a special effort to fit into the village,' she laughed in embarrassment at the memory; 'imagine that! You'd never believe it, would you? I made friends with other wives, I babysat for them, had them over to tea, chatted on about chickens, that sort of thing. It didn't work though because all the time I wanted to be alone. You'll probably understand what I mean since you were an only child!'

'I did spend a lot of time by myself. After a while I got used to being on my own,' I said supportively, wondering whether her childlessness was by choice or whether it was caused by Jack's abandonment of her.

'I just couldn't bear it after a while. He was always there, day in, day out, husbanding the poultry or husbanding me. And the women drove me mad with their company, and their children ran through my house breaking things. I craved for the days before I was married, before I gave my self to Jack. Sometimes I'd watch him as he slept, wanting to stab him to death. Isn't that awful! I was afraid of what I might do to him, poor thing!'

I laughed nervously at her confession. 'Why didn't you return to your parents, even if only for a bit of breathing space?'

'Because there's no going back once you've started out. I'm talking about the 1950s. It was expected you'd stay with your husband, otherwise people gossiped about your sanity or your morals. Anyway, it was my fault, not Jack's. He was solid, dedicated and industrious, I was the one who had inexplicable anxieties. I made the garden my sanctuary. I spent all my hours planting and pruning and uprooting, getting to know every blade of grass, every repetitive weed. I designed and redesigned it over the years, every spring and summer promised a new spectacle. I felt secure in the garden against all the disease outside. Poor Jack! Do you know that one season some mysterious disease killed every single chicken on the farm? He went about frantically poking needles into them, but the medicine failed, they didn't wake up. Another time all the eggs were somehow addled, no chick hatched, they all died in their shells.'

'Is that when he packed up and went to Africa?' I asked, piecing together the puzzle of their relationship. She had had enough however of talking and walked on.

When we reached the raised mound I paused, surveying the land, overwhelmed by its beauty in spite of Mrs Rutherford's assessment. Fields planted with wheat and barley, sheep fattening in the valleys and cottages garlanded in ivy were what I wanted to see. Only the sea was restless, pacing up and down the shore like a creature with toothache, reminding me of her talk of sickness.

'There's more wilderness here than Jack knew,' she resumed when we returned to her garden for late-morning refreshments. She wielded her scissors and lunged at the flowers while I sat on the patio, sipped tea and nibbled at a buttered scone. What an odd woman! I thought to myself as I watched her assaulting the roses. Bees, disturbed by her actions, swarmed angrily around her head, but she didn't seem to care, brushing off their threat with an occasional flourish of the scissors. The neatly laid lawn was decorated with shrubs, each artfully positioned to create a par-ticular effect. This spectacle of ordered beauty contrasted oddly with the violence she sought to project in her own figure. She's a mad Englishwoman, I decided, finishing my tea and giving up hope of resolving any of the contradictions of her character.

The day before, she had taken me on a tour of Hastings and we ended up in the Museum of Local History. After the usual exhibits of ancient flints and pottery we entered a room of glass cabinets containing a variety of stuffed fish – garpike, bow-fin, sturgeon, sharks and others with the most terrible spikes or teeth, all caught off the shore of Hastings. Even in death they were fearsome and the glass coffins added to their macabre appearance. I came upon a huge conger eel at least seven feet in length. Above was a black and white photograph of a woman standing beside a conger eel, which was hanging by its mouth from a scaffold. The woman wore a black Edwardian frock and she looked sober and matronly. A gaggle of boys, the children of the poor, surrounded her, gawping at the fish or at the camera. The photograph's caption told the scene in short bursts, as if trying to recapture the excitement of the moment: *World record. Miss Anna Hallett. Conger eel. Caught with rod and line. 64lbs 2oz. 27 Oct 1910.* I gazed at the picture and re-read the caption, wondering what the full story was, what the gaps between the staccato sentences told of this stern spinster-turned-fisherwoman posing calmly beside a monster she had dragged up from the depths of her own fantasy.

We emerged from the gloom and stillness of the museum into bright sunlight and pavements bristling with holiday-makers. 'Let's explore,' she suggested, taking me by the hand and leading me into a jeweller's shop. 'Ooh look,' she said excitedly, pointing to a string of pearls in one of the cabinets. 'What do you think?' She squeezed my hand, waiting for an opinion.

I looked at her neck, then at the pearls, uncertain of the correct response. 'It's probably too formal for you, too…'

'But I *am* formal,' she laughed, letting go of my hand.

'You'd look too… old in them,' I persisted, suddenly feeling embarrassed at my potential blunder.

'You're so kind,' she said smiling knowingly at me and brushing my cheek with her finger in mock affection. 'I'm old enough to be your mother. Those pearls suit me perfectly.' She looked at my face as if admiring its smoothness and its slight suggestion of hair. The jeweller cleared his throat to register his presence. Before I could say anything else she seized my hand and took me out into the adjoining shop. She tried on half a dozen pairs of shoes, hesitating each time before the mirror before sending them back. I noticed the smallness, almost daintiness of her feet, the softly creased flesh and slender toes that betokened a genteel existence. My own mother was mostly shoeless, except for church day, when she put on a pair that was still housed in its original box and placed neatly in the wardrobe. Her feet were stiff from years of tramping upon the hardened clay of the village road. The bunions had to be coaxed into her Sunday shoes and she walked to church in pain. She rested her hand occasionally on my shoulder as if to steady herself. 'Your father is my burden and wretchedness but you is my crutch,' she said when we arrived back home and she kicked off her shoes in relief. 'Now go do schoolwork and your sums and make your mother proud when you grow up.'

After trying out a few more shops Mrs Rutherford suddenly grew tired and wanted to rest awhile. We sat on the seafront eating ice-cream and watching the summer crowds stretching out on the beach to sunbathe. 'This is England,' she said between scoops, the gaiety draining from her face, 'England in all its mystery.' She scraped the wooden spoon sullenly along the bottom of the tub like a child disappointed to have to come to the end of its treat. 'If you want to know yourself and your colonial history, come to a seaside like this and behold! What pageantry of swimsuits and bathing trunks, what pennants on a battlefield! And the fat bodies, thin bodies, lumpy bodies, damp bodies, perfumed bodies, grey goose-pimpled bodies, all wanting to strip off and seek the sun, all swarming against each other for a piece of private beach. What's missing today of course are the polished black servants moving about bearing trays of iced refreshments. There's still a hint of the past in the treasure seekers,' she said pointing to a group of elderly men sweeping the sands with metal detectors. 'Do they do that on your beaches?'

'There's nothing on our beaches to dig up,' I said, thinking of the gold flashing from Swami's rotten jaw.

'Not even the bones of an eighteenth-century pirate?'

'Not really. The natives didn't put up resistance when they landed and the pirates didn't linger on the beach. They hurried towards the gold which was inland. The beaches are pure like most of the land. You can dig for days and come up with no evidence of previous humanity.'

'That's wonderful, truly wonderful,' she replied, gazing out at the half-naked crowd without seeing them. 'It was like that in Africa. I'd sit at the edge of the desert for hours and hours, delighted by the loneliness of everything. There were no herds of animals; each hunted on his own. When something stirred in the desert it was singular or it was a figment of your own mind. I learnt to wait and wait for the slightest movement or the slightest dot of rain. Then I'd hear Jack calling, "Janet! Janet! Janet!" He would come searching for me, terrified that some wild beast had dragged me off to its hole in the sand. "Janet!" he cried out and I would shudder awake, shudder at the strangeness of the English accent calling out in an African desert. "What the hell are you doing out here?" he would shout, "are you gone mad or what? I've been searching the earth for you." His face blistered with hatred and my calmness only made him more disturbed. Then I'd get up and go off with him, back to the familiarity of the English sound of my voice, back to myself as an English person in a certain place at a certain time with a certain mission, back to all that history. I just wanted the silence and the emptiness of the desert that Jack was making me leave behind.'

I stared into my tub of half-finished ice-cream rapidly melting in the heat, wanting to offer her a spoonful.

'But see, one of them has found something,' she exclaimed, deliberately breaking the thread of passion between us. I felt deeply and inexplicably bound to her. 'Probably some dagger or axehead,' she said, her mood turning sour again. 'They keep digging up all kinds of weapons on the beaches around here but none of them wants to see the horror. They only calculate the money value of their treasure, or else the blade that sliced somebody in two becomes part of our heritage; it takes on a certain glamour – the killer becomes historical and if the slaughter was substantial enough the council erects a plaque to attract more holiday-makers in future seasons. It's like those assorted dinosaur bones in the museum. Hundreds of them roamed around here, huge biting-machines, appallingly stupid things who only lived to kill. But all that horror is hidden away in the museum. We convert them into a special attraction for school-children who come armed with crayons to draw them. If only the bones could come alive and form the original beast you'd soon see the scramble. History would gobble them up and all their money-bags and plaques in one mouthful.' She chuckled at the thought of the pandemonium, the crowds screaming hysterically and mashing each other into the sand as they scattered for safety. 'Centuries from now someone could come along with metal detectors and retrieve *their* remains.'

'You think I'm a violent old woman don't you?' she said, pouring me a glass of rose-hip wine at the close of day. I was too tired to concoct a suitable answer. It had been a long day's tour of Hastings. Sitting under a hot sun for a couple of hours watching the crowds had drained me of energy. Mrs Rutherford though was bristling with life. It was as if all her earlier talk of monsters and murders had so charged her that sleep was impossible. 'Tell the truth now. You've been flattering me all day. You think I'm a strange old thing surrounded by stranger older things like those African carvings.'

'I've only recently arrived in your country, it's difficult to decide on anything,' I equivocated.

She scoffed at my weakness. 'Surely you've seen enough to hate England? Deep down you must hate the place and want to go home?'

'I've got my work to do here,' I replied, more than ever puzzled by her questions.

'Work, work, work, that's the doom of your people isn't it? Isn't that why the English shipped millions of you over to the Caribbean? So how come you don't hate them?'

'I've not really considered it that way... I just don't...' I said, thinking of Professor Fenwick's influence on me, his conscientious tuition and dedication to duty. How could I hate such a man, whatever culture he belonged to? A single act of kindness on his part had the power to erase a whole history of crime. 'It's the future that matters,' I continued, struggling to evolve a cogent answer, 'I'm *me*, not a mask or a movement of history. I'm not black, I'm an engineer.'

'That's silly,' she countered immediately, 'you can't block

yourself off from the past and sit daydreaming at the edge of a desert. That's why I had to go back with Jack, that's why I wanted him to find me even though I resented it. I walked away from the desert and returned to the English compound and began to fight. I really longed to be alone, colourless and invisible, but I couldn't escape being English, I couldn't escape being what I was. So I fought against myself. No more slushy reminiscences in the English Club about oak trees and cream teas back home. Of course the other women grew suspicious of me when I gave up bridge sessions and meetings to plan safari weekends. Jack made excuses for me, saying the heat had gone to my head, that I had become grumpy and solitary, but I didn't care. What mattered was secretly teaching the African children about our dinosaur culture, however deep we tried to bury it and make neat furrows and tranquil gardens in the earth above. Do you know that the best histories of England are being written by black scholars nowadays? Do you? Probably some of those very children I taught who have now grown up.' She snatched the glass from my hand and poured out more wine. I noticed the trace of froth at the corner of her mouth. She had worked herself up into a passion. I began to appreciate the reason for Jack's absence. He had not abandoned her, he had run away! She was too formidable for him, so he fled. All his fantasies of blood and sex were nothing compared to the knowledge of horror she possessed and was determined to proclaim. 'You don't know much about our history or yours,' she said, resuming her attack. 'Have you ever thought that the engineering you're versed in is all derived from us? That we've made you so whiter than white that whatever fear and hatred you should feel for us is covered over completely?'

The echo of Swami's accusation stung me into instant response. 'There's too much howling in this world, too much brokenness and muck. I just want to build my sea-dam.' The sudden emotion in my voice stilled her. 'It's clean – just me, stone and sea. When you're doing it you forget everything else, all the pain you've caused or others have. You believe totally in the task at hand. I don't believe in God, you see… there's no God. I don't ponder on what's just or unjust, I only trust my work.'

'Oh, but you do believe in God if you find solace in working rock and water. You're an African in spirit after all.' There was a hint of relief in her voice, as if the many hours of probing into my psyche had suddenly yielded a secret she had planted there in the first place. 'I must admit when you first came here I looked upon you suspiciously as a robot – something we had created, wound up and released into the world, a black man with an English soul. A black version of our King Canute, trying to beat back your passions. You spoke softly, with correct grammar, your consonants suppressed. The only hint of a deviant culture was in the roughness of your shirts. But I was wrong, you're an African deep down, but on the surface working with modern machines: a new breed of animist. You've managed to master the science and still retain a sense of nature, don't you think?'

Her assessment of me was hysterical and tedious. If anything it was she who was the animist, with her exaggerated worship of flowers. I felt more than ever exhausted by this relentless dredging-over of my being. Tomorrow would bring relief, a whole day working on my sea-defences, the screaming of the bulldozers distracting me from my humanity, drowning any feeling of remorse for past cruelties, any memory of shame or unfulfilment. I had found consolation before in the bulldozer's noise, when Swami died; the inhumane whining stifling the echoes of his words in my mind.

I stood on the lawn listening to the dog burrowing in the darkness as if he had caught scent of its monster. A faint thought crossed my mind that Jack was buried there, that Mrs Rutherford had killed and buried him beneath the beauty and serene art of her garden. The moon suddenly loosened from dense cloud and lit up the garden. The dog, startled by the abrupt illumination, stopped its burrowing under the cherry tree and hurried to my side.

SEVEN

Three weeks of wandering up and down the cliff with Mrs Rutherford came to an end and it was time to report for work. It was the first day of the month and it would be my first real day in England, I thought excitedly as I bathed and dressed. Mrs Ruther-ford was up earlier than usual as if she too recognised the special nature of the occasion. As she fussed at the table laying down toast and an assortment of honey and preserves I realised that it was an equally crucial day for her, the culmination of three weeks of grooming me for my entrance on the beach. She had taught me to name the flowers and she had warned me of the presence of corruption. I was to be cautious, discreet, self-protective, in the way she should have been in earlier years. She had complained and agitated instead, isolating herself from the villagers in Eng-land and the expatriates in Africa alike, making herself vulnerable to Jack's contempt and eventual separation. I was not to repeat the mistakes of her past. I was to be her emissary in the English world and her means of revenge. She had spent years preparing African children for such a role and the previous night I had put to rest all her qualms about my preparedness for victory. She had managed to convince herself that I was an African after all, and of special quality, since my spirit remained ancient (whatever that meant) in spite of my mastery of modern technology.

'Don't talk too much on your first day – not that you've shown yourself interested in prolonged conversation! But all the same be aware of yourself, even with Christie. He'll nod his head and distract you with his fool's bells but he's serious deep down. I could never fathom him beneath his child's play.' She gave my briefcase a quick polish, flicked a hair from my jacket and showed me to the door. As soon as it closed behind me I was overrun by nervousness. All Mrs Rutherford's careful pruning and snipping came to nought. I hesitated at the gate like a reluctant weed. For three weeks we had been married in passionate conversation and equally passionate silence. Even Jack had felt forsaken. He'd put on a pathetic face whenever he wandered into the sitting-room for a cuddle only to be ignored by Mrs Rutherford, who was making some intense revelation to me. When she closed the door behind me I knew Jack's misery. I was alone, abandoned. Only the memory of my mother's grief upon hearing of my father's desertion prodded my feet forward. 'What to do?' she said when she ceased crying and reached automatically for her duster. 'Is God's will, howsoever spiked and pitch-black. What to do but repent and get back to cleaning God's house?'

I made my way along the cliff-top path she and I had trodden so frequently but which now seemed unfamiliar in her absence. As I pushed through the wild brambles I was more than ever convinced that she was mad. I was not the black white knight she wanted me to be. Still, I paused to pick a flower, a solitary purple thing that poked its head out of the bush as if to spy my progress on behalf of Mrs Rutherford. I didn't know its name but I hoped it was something horrible like toadflax or lousewort, which would please her. I put it in my pocket like a lover's memento and descended the cliff.

I was stared at as soon as I approached the camp. Even the bulldozers seemed to cease their whining. It was to be expected. A black man in a striped suit and shiny briefcase walking an English beach at the crack of dawn was bound to be as barbarous a sight as the Normans and Danes who appeared bearing axes in previous centuries. Professor Fenwick in his naïve goodness had obviously not alerted them to my nature. To be truthful I was the one prickling with fear. The workmen were huge, tattooed, rough-looking creatures whose skin shone grey and ghostly in the half-light. I was accustomed to my frail coolies. I was glad of the protection of the talismanic flower in my pocket. I went up to one of them and asked shyly for Mr Rushton, the Site Manager. The creature said nothing and stood his ground. He looked me up and down as if examining himself in the mirror and finding the reflection too appalling for words. 'Mr Rushton,' I repeated quietly, but he still didn't budge. I felt like some prehistoric bone in the Hastings Museum which had suddenly stirred in its glass cabinet, stunning the observer into speechlessness. Another workman came over as if to fortify his mate. He had a smile on his face which I took for a token of friendship, so I redirected my enquiry to him. He replied in a tongue I couldn't follow, an English so mangled and accented that I knew immediately that it was Irish and that the man before me was Christie. His ease with me suggested that he had met my kind before, perhaps on sea voyages, for his wrinkled face and stubbled chin somehow suggested a life aboard ships. Sensing that I could not understand him, he began to gesture, inventing a sign language on the spot. I could not bring myself to respond in like manner, so I reached for my pocket and offered him my card. Mrs Rutherford had had the foresight to order some from a Hastings printer, buying me the leather briefcase and sober tie at the same time. The workman squinted at it in what I took to be a sign of illiteracy. It was only when he handed the card back to me that I noticed that the wet purple flower had stained the print beyond legibility.

'Mr Rushton is away – ill; I guess you must be from the agency,' he said chirpily, 'seeing you've got on a suit and all.' He led me to an office, a prefabricated white box perched on a platform of concrete blocks. 'I don't suppose you're from these parts,' he said, stirring milk into a cup of coffee he'd poured out from his own flask and handing it to me.

'No, and nor are you by the sound of it,' I said. He looked surprised, the feigned joviality slipping from his face. 'You must be Christie,' I said, offering him my hand. He looked at it, even more surprised.

'How do you know?'

'Someone in the village told me about you.'

'I'm Christie all right,' he said, reasserting the authority of his self. 'I'm a foreigner, from Ireland.' He rolled a cigarette from a pouch of tobacco and offered it to me. He embarked upon a long tale about his previous life and the various adventures that had brought him to this beach. He kept gesticulating as if the story couldn't be told without being woven simultaneously by his hands. 'How I ended up here Jesus only knows!' he concluded, spitting out a grain of tobacco in a volley of self-disgust. 'My only experience of the sea before this was the ferry crossing between Dun Laoghaire and Holyhead. I had threw up all the way. The family had a farewell fuck-up in the local beforehand, if you get my French, I staggered on to the ship merrier than an old maid granted her one wish three times by the leprechaun.' The cultural allusion passed me by, the difficulty compounded by the strangeness of his accent. 'It's a creature that keeps popping up from wayside bushes and makes magic for you,' he explained thoughtfully. 'There must be millions of them in your place, seeing how your folk are more primal like, from the Third World and all. No offence meant mind you. Sure I can tell you're a right Christian gentleman just by looking.' He pointed to my briefcase, impressed by official documents it must contain. 'What do you do then, sir, if I may call you that?'

'I'm an engineer trained in Guyana. I've only just come here, three weeks ago, Professor Fenwick's instruction,' I said firmly, trying to assert some authority in Mr Rushton's absence. He was put off by my sternness, but quick as a flash he became jovial again.

'Well, isn't that fine, isn't that just grand. You'll love it here, the fresh air, the seaside. There's people that would give their right arm to walk along these beaches all day, honest.' He seemed to have run out of conversation, having told me in one long uninterrupted burst of speech his total life story. Yet he lingered in the office, either curious to find out more about me or out of reluctance to resume work, seeing that Mr Rushton was away for the day. 'Guyana eh? A far place it sounds like. Where's that exactly?'

'On the coast of South America, on top of Brazil.'

'Is that so now? Oh yes, that's right, yes, Brazil.' He nodded vigorously as if to signal intimacy with the geography. 'Are there no leprechauns in your part of the world then?' he asked innocently.

'What?' I replied vaguely, not quite hearing the question. I had been looking out of the window while he chatted on, anxious to see what work was being done in the absence of supervisors.

'Leprechauns,' he repeated, throwing my attention back to his history. It was as if the only topic of conversation he could start with me related to his suspicion of my paganism. He could only

100

connect with me on the level of the primitive. He suddenly leapt out of his chair, crouched, grinned, did a little wriggle and held up three fingers in an impersonation of a leprechaun's behaviour. Was it part of the Irish character to make signs, I wondered, or did he take me for a dumb creature? He was a sign in himself, his rough face and hands and muscles that swelled his arms like a deformity, telling of years of labour borne out of desperation. He had said that hunger and violence had driven him to England to seek employment, as previous generations of his people had done.

'We call them Jumbies,' I said.

'Jumbies, eh? Jumbies. That's a good one. Nice name that. And what kind of magic do they work?'

'Black through and through,' I said gravely, going along with his game, partly to see what foolishness it would lead to, partly because I was unsure how much of it was masquerade and how much serious. In any case a moment of levity could do no harm to my relationship with the workmen. Swami had urged me to ease up, to become more irreverent.

If he was being playful before, testing me out for evidence of primitivism, his mood now changed. He appeared alarmed by the tone of my voice and eyed me cautiously. He seemed prepared to go back to work instantly, and cast a glance at the beach, seeking reassurance that his mates were still recognisable and not metamorphosed into crabs. 'That's nice, Jumbies, nice one,' he said bravely, deciding to put up a fight. He sat solidly again in his chair. He would not let the side down and depart nervously. 'You must have heard of the spirits of Connemara,' he said looking me in the eye, 'bloody great evil flapping things that would swoop down and bite off the heads of English soldiery. Bloody world-famous they are, you must have heard of them.' He wriggled his fingers in his ear as if loosening the wax to improve my own hearing.

'I've heard of Dublin but not Connemara and never about spirits.'

'Aye, there you are, you've got it,' he said leaning back in his chair. 'The spirits moved to Dublin and devastated the English garrisons there. That was the famous year of 1848 when the whole world from Edinburgh to London trembled at the news of slaughter. It must have reached your parts too.'

I screwed up my face in an attitude of mock pensiveness then gave in. '1848 rings a bell but I can't say I know much about the world history. We're a small place really and the people are parochial; they don't follow the world news in a dedicated way. Even the Jumbies are local.'

He looked genuinely relieved. 'How do you mean?' he asked.

'Well, your lot seem to terrorise at a national level whereas ours tend to create havoc in small places – a single house or a village at the most. And unlike your leprechauns ours tend to maim or kill rather than gratify a wish. They come in all kinds, each a specialist in one particular horror.' Christie listened intensely and when I paused he signalled me on. I told him of Bakoo, Ole Higue, Sukhanti and other spirits, giving him some of the ghastly details. 'The worst is Swami,' I concluded, lowering my head as if affected by some dreadful memory of this being.

'Swami?' he asked, offering me another cigarette.

'Yes, Swami. He kills by drowning. He makes the sea rush in and sweep away whole villages and towns.' I stopped there, bored with the cat-and-mouse game of superstitions. He hesitated in the hut, then, realising I was determined to end our conversation, decided to join the gang on the beach. An hour had passed and I was anxious to get started, but without Mr Rushton's presence I was at a loss as to what to do.

'Why don't you go home and come back tomorrow,' Christie suggested, sensing my lack of direction, 'there's nothing much happening today anyway. The English workers are thinking of a strike because Rushton decided to shave a few minutes off the tea-break. Not that it makes a bit of difference. You'll soon find out for yourself that things are slow around here. The only ones who work are the Irish. They've been at it for centuries, they're the leprechauns of England, the ones who get things done by miracles. The rest just look busy.'

I lingered in the hut all day, reluctant to walk among the workers. They sat around in small groups doing nothing. A few had spread towels on the sand and were sunbathing. One or two appeared to be busy, taking measurements of the contour of the beach. A bulldozer banked sand at the toe of the cliff and the crane swayed here and there, bearing bundles of girders. Thousands of rocks were piled on the foreshore. Eventually they would be sorted out by size and arranged to form a sea-wall of even height but for the moment they lay in a huge neglected heap. The seaweed and slime greening the granite suggested that they had been lying there for some time. I searched Rushton's desk for a schedule of works but could find nothing. In the top drawer were a few charts outlining the work to be done but no timetable. The charts were roughly drawn and badly kept, stained in places where Rushton had rested his coffee mug. The bottom drawer was empty apart from pieces of silver foil in which he had wrapped his sandwiches. I was quietly distressed by the untidiness of the whole scene, the lack of purpose and absence of authority. As it was my first day at work I decided that I would restrain myself and say nothing to the workers who kept coming into the office to use the telephone. They all looked at me warily, giving me the slightest of nods, hardly speaking a word and leaving the hut as soon as they could. Christie had obviously depicted me as a witch-doctor of dangerous talents. It was curious to think that the spirit of Swami was still moving among us. Perhaps my authority with the workers would ultimately rest with my supposed intimacy with Swami. I would terrify them into diligence by mere evocation of his name and hint of punitive rituals, a latter-day Prester John casting a huge black seductive shadow on an English beach. To their mind I was savage beneath my suit, and my briefcase really contained strange herbs. When I was alone, doubtless I dropped my impeccable English speech and howled.

I made my way home knowing that I had let Mrs Rutherford down. She had spent all that time preparing me for my encounter with her people but instead of imposing authority over them by my polished and learned presence I had fed them mumbo-jumbo. Christie's ploy of appearing to be superstitious in order to bring out my own backwardness had succeeded. All the time he had been establishing a sense of his own superiority over me. Why, I wondered, did I feel the need to appear exotic before the whites, when I should have been my true self, a trained engineer, a dedicated scientist? I had learnt as a boy that there were no spirits but those devised by my own imagination. I had spent three days in utter solitude on the shore and had seen nothing that I could report to Mr Roosevelt. Roosevelt knew I was lying about the crabs and the iguana because he knew that he was a liar himself. His travels abroad had yielded no marvels. That he made them up was a measure of his ambitiousness and his deepest wish to prod a younger mind to fulfil those ambitions. He would labour in his hut until he dropped dead, but I was to move beyond the dirt road of the village to prospect faraway lands, to find the magical wealth he doubted existed. Years later I did journey to listen to scientific papers in the very islands he claimed he had visited, islands which the early European imagination had deemed to be El Dorado. I saw nothing but endless stretches of cane-fields and bare-backed men hacking in them. The women Roosevelt claimed possessed utmost glamour turned out to be foul-mouthed and fat with excessive child-bearing. In the market-places they squatted lethargically before trays of mangoes or pumpkins, waking up only to haggle plaintively with shoppers or curse them when they refused to buy. Cities were a tawdry conglomeration of concrete and steel, banks and government offices which were the showpiece buildings of these independent states. Huge banners were draped from lampposts, each bearing the rhetoric of the rulers, exhorting the masses to produce more and cheaply: THE SMALL MAN IS THE NATION'S TREASURE, PATRIOTISM BEGINS AT THE WORKPLACE, and so on. The highways were new and shiny, cutting through the landscape in grandiose sweeps of pitch, but there were few vehicles plying their broad lanes. Their excess and expense told of the vision of the rulers: one day these ragged outcrops of rock rising out of the sea would be the hubs of global industries, drawing to their centres international statesmen, businessmen and other people of extreme significance. I sought refuge in the conference-room from such hyperactivity of nationalist fantasy, concentrating in as calm a manner as possible on the ways I could balance the elements, organising mud, wattle, brick, timber and stone to control the flow of water.

I arrived home in a dejected mood and went to my room to bathe. To my surprise Mrs Rutherford had laid out a freshly laundered shirt on the bed, and this simple act of kindness helped banish the gloom from my mind. I could see from tell-tale marks on the glass that she had even polished my mother's photograph which stood on the mantelshelf. I washed the salt and sand from my body, put on clean clothes and went downstairs to be greeted by her bright smile, a pot of tea and home-made cakes. She sat me down and busied herself serving the treat she had planned for me the moment I had left the house. We sat opposite each other and ate quietly, exchanging no more than a few pleasantries. I could sense the affection with which she viewed me. Afterwards she cleared the table and directed me to the sitting-room, a routine we were to follow undeviatingly in the months I spent with her. It was as if the hours had to be clearly demarcated and certain rituals observed so as to impose a restraint between us, a distance in which we could confess the most passionate hurts covertly.

'The wind is unusually strong this evening,' she said casually, handing me a glass of wine.

'It is rather strong,' I agreed, taking it from her.

'I think I'll bake us a huge pie tomorrow, what do you say?' She leant back in her chair and sipped from her glass. 'You can share it with your colleagues on the beach,' she continued, steering the conversation to my day's work. 'I'm sure you must have made lots of friends already.'

'Not really, I was mostly busy… taking measurements and familiarising myself with the equipment.'

'Oh,' she said, a hint of suspicion in her voice, 'I should have thought you would spend your first day getting to know the people, finding out what they've been up to.'

'I did have a friendly chat with Christie.'

'There you are! It wasn't all work then. And what did he have to say for himself?'

'Not much. He mentioned the traumas of being Irish.'

'Did he talk about me at all?'

'No,' I said, curious again as to what Christie would have spoken about Mrs Rutherford.

'Did he mention Mr Curtis?'

'No, but Professor Fenwick told me to check him out. How do I go about meeting him?'

She didn't answer, switching the conversation back on to

Christie. 'Christie's confirmed in his belief that I am a witch. He called into the house one Christmas with a bottle of sherry and leant towards me for a festive kiss. His eyes must have caught the masks behind me for he suddenly stiffened, downed his glass and scooted off – more a stagger really, a mixture of alcohol and fright. All his joky talk of spirits suddenly confronted him in the masks and he no longer wanted to seduce me. He's a bit of a womaniser, old Christie is. Jack never liked it when he came to the house and I was alone with him. Jack would sulk away and fret by himself until I called him for his dinner.' She chuckled to herself, remembering some pleasurable detail of her past. 'Christie must have told you ghost stories as well.'

I nodded in guilt and shame.

'He swears that the village is supernatural, that many of the old women are inhabited by the spirits of all those gorgeous young maidens they used to burn around here in the fourteenth century, many of them barely on the brink of puberty. According to Christie, the men used to round them up as witches, drag them to Romney Marsh, put them through all kinds of trials and humiliations before torching them. The odd thing is that a lot of women used to attend the killings, howling their men on. I suppose they were envious of younger bodies than theirs, bodies they once possessed before their men got on top of them. The women didn't want their men to be reminded of youthful female flesh, or perhaps they didn't want to be reminded either. So they darkened their past, reducing it to skin burnt beyond recognition. From what Christie says Dunsmere might as well be a village in the Congo.'

'But why does Christie think that the old women in the village have been taken over?' I asked, hoping to find the source of Mrs Rutherford's own passionate and unstable character.

'Well it's the way they behave. Just look at Mrs Goldsmith. She's totally gone in the head, sunbathing naked in her garden, which backs onto the cliffs. The garden is surrounded by high hedges and the closest neighbour is too far away to peep, but there's always the coastguard's helicopter, she hopes. As soon as there is a storm or the prospect of drowned swimmers, out goes Mrs Goldsmith, peels off her clothes and stretches out in the grass waiting for the helicopter to hover over. If she looks as ghastly a sight from the air as she does from land it's a wonder the pilot doesn't crash.' She paused for breath and drank some more wine greedily. There was an intensity in her eyes bordering on disorder. Her hair suddenly looked unkempt, the sagging flesh around her chin became a sign of debauchery. 'Oh well,' she sighed, leaning back and relaxing as abruptly as she had wound herself into a frenzy. The kindliness returned to her face, she was once more the rugged but generous spirit I had come to know in the time I had lived under her roof. 'I must admit I do like Christie and all his superstitions,' she said, turning to me and smiling; 'at least he senses that there are deep-down things in this village, that it's not all rabbits sitting up in tall grass. He's not like Jack, who took it all with masturbatory and adolescent seriousness. Christie is only half joking, he hides his real hurt.'

EIGHT

Mr Rushton, despite my expectations, turned out to be a quietly efficient man. He greeted me politely when I showed up the next day, apologising for his illness. He took me on an inspection tour of the site, introducing me to groups of workers without the least hint of embarrassment at my strangeness. He spoke in brief clipped sentences when he gave them instructions and in such a soft voice that he was barely audible. I noticed that he never used personal pronouns when speaking, as if he was accustomed to keeping a distance between himself and his fellow men. It was not that he studiously avoided intimacy: he was completely at ease in his manner, years of accomplished work giving him such authority that there was no need to shout or appeal to his men personally. To begin with, his lowered tone of voice and the way he broke off in mid-sentence to start another made me think that his mind was full of all kinds of secrets – if he wasn't careful he would blurt them out untidily. As time went on however I began to appreciate that it was as a result of a self-assurance based on mastery of his craft, a self-assurance so complete that it made him matter-of-fact. The workers were stiffly respectful in his presence but as soon as he turned his back they seemed to slouch and grow aimless. I would watch them out of the window of my cabin, wandering around the piles of rocks or digging holes in the sand, seemingly without purpose. I wondered how Mr Rushton could operate efficiently and according to schedule and what the foundations of his previous achievements were, given what I had heard from Christie of the laziness of English workers. In Guyana I would have gone out and bullied them, threatening to withhold pay or this or that privilege. Mr Rushton however sat calmly in his cabin, jabbing away at the calculator for most of the day and reading the figures down the phone to company headquarters. 'A bit slow,' he agreed, reading my thoughts and pointing to the men. He immediately resumed pressing the buttons on the machine as if his index finger was better employed in that task rather than gesturing angrily at the workforce. He seemed as reconciled to their habits as to the numbers he computed. At the end of the day he tidied up the office, stuffing all loose pieces of paper in the two drawers of his desk. He went home, his mind spick and span, untroubled by thoughts of unfinished work or possible mishaps in the future which would demand sleepless nights and detailed planning now. As I watched him go I questioned my previous methods in Guyana. Perhaps I failed and the sea poured in because I was too excited by my work, cursing the coolies, impatient with Mr Pearce's lust and lethargy. What was needed was not control of the elemental ghosts Swami spoke of but control of one's passionate self, one's own humanity. To Mr Rushton the sea was a machine vaster than any the human imagination could conceive, so he had reconciled himself to the calculations he could make on his hand-sized machine which only needed a digit, his finger, to activate. If he were to allow himself to dwell on the imponderable mass of the sea his finger would slip and cause havoc. So he shrank his mind to the dimensions of the calculator, believing in nothing but numbers that added up. As he disappeared round the corner of the cliff I wondered what outlet he found for the magic bottled up in him. Would he go home and beat his wife or dress up in women's clothing or paint or get drunk? Did he ever uncork himself in private acts of cruelty and fantasy? I found myself puzzling over his character, as fifteen years before, in identical circumstances, I had questioned the restraint of Professor Fenwick. Was it because they could rule their spirits that they once ruled the seas and made an Empire? But what now that the cliffs around Hastings were collapsing as the Empire had crumbled? What need for rigidities now that their own people had grown work-shy and purposeless? Did Professor Fenwick and Rushton think upon these matters and then settle on a solution: to be flexible to their workforce but maintain a shell of authority by adherence to figures? Surely the shell, however rigid, could not withstand the weight of the workers' lethargy? But perhaps it could, like the shells littering the beach which survived the most crushing force of the sea. Certainly Fenwick had endured the rigours of a post-imperial Guyana. The nature of his survival suddenly dawned on me: he had a relaxed attitude to the character of the native yet held steadfastly to his engineering computations. We had seen substance in him when we should have seen the shell of Empire. Swami was right after all: we were bound to fail because we didn't have the confidence to believe we could make our own computations without benefit of whites like Fenwick. We trusted entirely in his methods, ruling the land in grids. The sea flooded in because we had no intimacy with the land, and we scoffed at Swami's stories of Churile, Sukhanti and other ghosts.

Christie appeared, as if summoned up by my musings on the laziness of white workers and the hollowness of their managers. 'Christie, how long have you people been working at this site? Tell me honestly.' I was desperate to see the outline of a sea-wall.

'About three months, why?'

'Well, everything seems so blasted disorganised! I can't see a beginning or an end. Machines and rocks are dumped haphazardly, as if no one is concerned with the pace and direction of the work.'

'Steady on,' Christie laughed, 'just don't let Rushton hear you talking like that. What's the great hurry? We have until December before the sea grows stormy.'

'But December is only a few months off. There are at least ten thousand rocks of different weight and size that need careful placing.'

'Well we've spent weeks digging a proper foundation in the sand. It all takes time you know.'

'Yes, but excavating foundations in these conditions and with all these efficient machines should take no more than four or five weeks. In Guyana we'd achieve more with picks.'

'People here are not slaves you know,' he chided me. 'It's all right in your country to beat them into the ground and shovel dirt over them. You've got to realise we are men of dignity. Your lot may rush into things all wild-limbed and wrong-headed. Here we devise a system, and then an alternative system in case the first one don't work, and then a back-up system for the alternative system. That's why Rushton is calculating all day – the number of gangs, who's in charge of whom, how many hours they work a day, how long they rest, how many shifts, what rates of pay they get, what bonuses, what holidays, and that's only the men. You've got machines to look after, how long we can afford to lease them, the cost of repairs and maintenance and so on and so forth. It's big business. Rushton must have had to get ten years' learning before he could know how to quantify. That's why he's the boss and I've got blisters and a meagre pay-packet in my hand.'

'I know all that,' I said impatiently, refusing to give him sympathy, 'I'm a trained man myself.'

He took offence at my outburst. 'There's no call for you to be so superior. I know I'm nothing, an Irish peasant, but I don't call you a coon so why put me down. If you don't like it you could always go back home.'

He turned to walk away but I caught him by the arm and steadied him. 'I didn't mean to cause offence and I'm sorry if I did,' I lied.

He looked me directly in the eye to assess my honesty. 'OK. No offence taken,' he said, shoving his hand abruptly towards me. I shook it and he patted me on the back. 'You see, you're foreign,' he said in a tone of friendship and reconciliation. 'You just have to get used to the way we do things around here. It's all down to your union and the union has got rules. If everybody was to work as hard as you want them to they would grow ill and then it's about compensation, which the bosses want to avoid because it's expensive. A broken arm is worth a few thousand quid, a lost thumb twice that. Any injury below the waist is a jackpot. The bosses can't take chances so we take it easy.'

'But isn't it all a pretence for not doing real work? You yourself told me they were an indolent bunch.'

'Yes but it's all right for *me* to say it. I'm still one of us, Irish or not. You should just keep quiet and keep out of it, otherwise there's no place for you here.' He looked vexed, as if confiding in me had given me power over his people. 'By the way, you didn't tell me you were staying at that old dragon's house,' he said,

111

puffing smoke in my face. His remark offended me. It was embarrassing to hear Mrs Rutherford described in such an insulting manner. 'That's all right, my friend,' he continued, sensing that I was about to rally to her defence, 'she has that effect on all the men.' He looked at me and grinned. 'Take me as a nice example. There I used to go to her house, innocent like, every Sunday lunchtime to help with the garden. Green fingers you know, all the Irish have them. "Hello Christie," she'd greet me and right away a cup of tea and some nibbles. Jack was in the pub all the time reading the papers. Odd that, the way he liked to be by himself. He'd sit in a crowded pub and hide himself behind the papers – he bought the ones with the longest and widest pages – so as not to talk to anyone.'

'What did he look like?' I asked, my curiosity about him aroused once more.

'More handsome than you, so you've need to be jealous of him and Mrs Rutherford.'

'Come, Christie, give me a straight answer.' He was surprised by the eagerness of my voice.

'Well, he was just a bloke, like other blokes. Now let me see… he was white, that's for sure. He had your profile. In fact if you wasn't so black, on a dark night I'd swear you was him. Then he was tall… wait, I tell a lie, he was medium height. An ordinary nose. Ordinary eyes, grey-blue I think and… ordinary hair, that's about it.' When I expressed disappointment at his poor description he huffed and blew more smoke in my direction. 'I'm not a terrorist, only a common labourer. What would I want to know about photofits. Jack was normal I tell you, like you and me.' I waved him on to resume his story. 'Come to think of it he was a shade too normal, you know, drinking only a pint, no more, never swearing, working ever so hard to make a success of the farm. You'd never suspect that a man like that could be up to anything out of the ordinary. In fact it's Janet who set him on edge. If it wasn't for her he'd be a perfectly sane and respectable bloke… anyway as I was saying, I'd drink the tea, and then another, and off I'd go to the herb garden to plant chives and sweet cicely and mint and parsley. Just to give her a hand mind you, good-neighbour-liness, that's all there was, I swear, even though she was younger then, a sweet-faced Englishwoman who talked so pretty about flowers. Not a foul word fell from her lips in those days. She was fresh-breathed and I was glad to work freely for her.' He paused and stared at the end of the cigarette, uncertain as to whether to stub it out. 'The men in the village fancied her, I swear, all of them, except me,' he resumed, taking a final deep drag and flinging it out of the window. 'I bet she didn't even know, that's how innocent she was. Or at least she behaved all innocent. Who's to know women? Who's to know what she was up to when Jack was working on the farm?'

'How long ago was that?' I asked, brushing aside his insinuation, wanting instead to date her beauty.

'Oh let me see now, I'd say thirty years or so, in the '50s. She was truly lovely. All the wives were burning with envy, they guarded their men from her. I can tell you a thing or two about how they hated her! But she was serene, she never spread gossip about them, if anything she went out of her way to be charitable, baking cakes for the children and all. But she was always the outsider, the strange one from somewhere else who was struggling to belong. Loneliness was written all over her. Then Jack took her away to Africa, away from all our gazes. When she came back she was tired and cracked, the sun had dried her like a river bed. No more greetings flowed from her. She rarely ventured out in the village and the hedge around her garden grew taller each year, walling her in. When I walked past the house and saw her at the gate I'd wave and mumble a few words but she only scowled and turned away. I could almost hear her curse beneath her breath. She'd become an old crotchety witch. No wonder Jack picked up and left. He had no need to be jealous of her any more.'

'Was Jack a jealous man then?'

'Jealous? Are you asking me whether he was jealous?' He laughed.

'I thought you said he was even-tempered and ordinary.'

'Yes, but she moved him to passion, I can tell you. One Sunday it was so hot I had to take off my shirt. I sat in the shade of the cherry tree taking a break. She came up to me with a cup of tea and as she bent over to hand it to me, who walks into the garden unexpectedly but Jack. He had come home earlier than usual, as if he could smell the sweat on my naked chest all the way in the pub. He glared at her and she went straight away into the house with him. I could hear him screaming at her. Then he must have hit her because everything went quiet. Afterwards he came out and ordered me out of his property. Of course I could have beaten the shit out of him, but I went quietly in case he took it out on her later. Also I didn't want to kill him with one surprise of a blow. He had a rotten heart you know, all that smoking. That's why he could never work on the farm for long stretches – he'd huff and puff as if he was trying for an erection.'

'So you never swaggered up to her drunk one Christmas and tried to kiss her?' I asked, ignoring his vulgarity.

'Who, me? Never. I swear I never. Don't get me wrong, it's not that I'm a gentleman, it's just that I'd never dare to affront her. I should have tried really, shouldn't I?' He drifted into a mood of regret then woke up with a vengeance. 'A right bitch she can be when you dwell on it! She would have given favours to all the men of the village but not me. I'm too humble you see, a mucky Irishman, what can you expect? Her with her tidy garden and English graces, I bet Jack had every reason to be nasty. There were all kinds of rumours about her, especially with that Mr Curtis. I can't imagine what fun she would have got from him though – the man is as picturesque as a pile of stones.'

Christie seemed willing to open up, unlike Mrs Rutherford, who had mentioned the name of Mr Curtis only in the briefest of allusions as if he was a mere afterthought in the conversation. When I first arrived she had given me detailed biographies of some of the villagers – 'culprits and scamps', she called them, the people I should watch out for – but Mr Curtis had only the most guarded of introductions. It was always 'the teasels by Mr Curtis's house' or 'So-and-so has a lawnmower louder than Mr Curtis's'; he was always introduced by reference to objects as if he had no personal identity.

'Curtis was the one for her, I can tell you.' He hesitated, sensing the urgency of my curiosity and weighing up in his mind whether or not to keep me on edge, out of spite. 'All right then, what do you want to know?' he relented, a generous grin on his face. 'You're as foreign as me, I might as well show you how people do things around here. Ask me anything, go on.' The way he squared up before me to give his body authority reminded me of Swami. I wondered whether I would be spun another web of insubstantial tales.

'Who exactly is Curtis? Was he married to Mrs Rutherford?'

'Is that all?' he asked in mock disappointment, 'so you don't want to hear about her dirty secret sex-life? Marriage, eh? That's a fine word for it that is!'

'All right then, tell me the dirt if that's all there is to it,' I conceded, betraying my instinct to protect Mrs Rutherford from calumny, as I would have protected the reputation of a mother or lover. Christie looked at me pitifully as though I had sunk to his level; as if my professional, groomed appearance disguised a prurience as base as his.

'You're like all of them, aren't you?' he said accusingly, 'and you coming from so far away! You should know better. Don't your culture have decency then, or is it like what we have here?'

'Of course we have decency,' I replied, but he wasn't listening. He began to mutter to himself about how he had hoped that there was some part of the world where people didn't dishonour and abuse each other. It was as if I had betrayed some deep expectation in him. He sounded like Swami and Alfred, discontented with the spot they inhabited, dreaming of other places of superior value. His voice suddenly flared with anger and he went on the offensive again.

'You should watch yourself, wanting to know white people's affairs. In America they'd string you up for peeping under a white woman's skirt. We do things different here, but you're still black so don't forget it.'

'Don't be ridiculous! It was you who started all this vulgarity. And who'd dare lynch me? You?' I asked, losing my temper in turn.

'The trouble with you is the same trouble with Curtis and that whore Janet Rutherford. You all think you're a better kind, knowing everything, but you only rub people up the wrong way. Compared to us you're a real waste of skin.' He flexed his muscles as if contemplating as assault upon me, but I looked steadily into his face and he surrendered. He was much larger than me so perhaps it was my previous talk of Jumbies that kept him in check. Either that or he had decided that I was not worth his attention, as he had claimed Mrs Rutherford held no attraction for him.

'I bet you they all had her, Curtis and every man Jack around here when she was young, before she went to Africa,' he taunted me, suddenly blasting her character, contradicting all his previous testimony of her virtue. 'She'll have nothing left for you. All she'll give you is some story about her days in the Empire. But the Empire's done, and all the excitement, and so is she. Flab and superannuation and dull old stories is all she's got, and a house that'll surely crash into the sea. Don't think you can save her from what's coming to her.'

NINE

I didn't bother to dwell on Christie's outburst as I walked home.
Like Mrs Rutherford I decided he was a piece of pageantry,
something picturesque and marginal called 'Irish'. He caught my
attention though, unlike the characterless and invisible English
people of the village. I was beginning to become bored with
England, its dull tranquillity, its duller prejudices. Whatever
excitements its past held – of conquest and mission – had largely
disappeared. The village was lifeless waxwork after all, and I
found myself maliciously waiting for the next slippage of cliff-
face, which would at least be loud enough to make cracks in the
wax and stir people into alarmed conversation.

I passed their cottages on my way from the cliff, glancing
furtively at their doorways. I hurried by out of guilt over all the
intimate information I had amassed on the occupants. They were
probably peeping out of their windows at me, without realising
that I was no stranger to their lives. They assessed me by my
surface, my skin colour and the quality of my suit, but although
they were hidden from me I knew what they looked like inside.
I knew the mean from the wasteful, the sober from the lecherous.
I knew whom they were married to, divorced from, how much
wealth they had acquired and by what means, where they took
their holidays and how often, even the names of their dogs and
cats. Such knowledge however gave me no power over them, as
Mrs Rutherford hoped. I had no belief that I could connect with
them. Their lives were as foreign as the flowers Mrs Rutherford
introduced me to. After a few weeks I could name the flowers as
I could name the sins of the villagers but I felt that I could still not
inhabit the place. It was simply not mine. The hills, the fatted

sheep, the cottages, the pub, the church, the language preserved and spoken, the manner of dressing body or meat, the gestures made, the looks exchanged, none of these were intrinsic to me. Mrs Rutherford had explained that black people living in Britain were discriminated against in many ways. Laws should be passed, she argued, to give equality to them. They are after all British citizens. I felt though that equality could only work rapidly in cities, which were random, chaotic places, allowing people to dissolve into each other. Cities contained little memory of the past except for a handful of venerable stone buildings surviving precariously among concrete and glass constructions of an international style. Nor were the rituals of nationhood enacted in cities, apart from the odd procession put on for sheer pageantry. Rural Dunsmere was entirely different. It would take centuries for a hybrid flower to evolve, slowly transformed by pollen from the east brought back by Crusaders and merchant venturers. At first I had felt, as a West-Indian, that I could easily rest here, or anywhere, but the masks had unsettled me, by their evocation of an ancient specific order to which I was involuntarily bound. The villagers watching me behind their curtains knew this. They saw on the surface of my face the testimony of the masks, and they hid or kept to themselves, partly out of fright, partly out of realisation that I was so different from them that I might as well be invisible. After a while, when they got over the shock of my appearance, they looked hard at me and quite possibly saw nothing. Even if I smiled or screamed, my face would remain in their minds as alien and imperturbable as the expression on the masks. It was not that they ignored me, it was just that there was nothing to acknowledge. As to Mrs Rutherford, did she really belong to Africa as she claimed, or was she not a tourist like Jack? Were not both of them merely savouring the apparent excitements of Africa, Jack feeding his sexual fantasies and Mrs Rutherford her anger at being an Englishwoman?

It was in such crisis that I turned a corner of the cliff-top and suddenly caught sight of the sea again. All confusion was relieved, all disquieting thoughts about how I could belong or not belong. Here was something more restless than myself, belonging no-where and everywhere, having no uniform shape or colour, constantly changing upon itself yet remaining the same. Nor could it be confined by the dogmas of history. It was older than any measurement that man could make and it negated even recent events which sought to give it history. Each new wave was a previous page turned over and forever dissolved. It kept no archive of the ships that brought us from Africa. We existed and then never existed, giving way to other peoples and other disappearances. I was seduced by its endless transformations, which promised me freedom from being fixed as an African, a West-Indian, a member of a particular nationality of a particular epoch. The stories of my personal life could easily be extinguished in its mass. The brutal mechanical noise it made as it steamrolled towards the shore could easily obliterate the human voices in my head. And yet I wanted to be somebody, not any thing, and resisted the sea's indiscriminateness. When Mrs Rutherford asked me why I became an engineer I couldn't answer, but deep down I knew a dam was my identity, an obstacle I sought to put between shore and sea to assert my substantialness, my indissoluble presence, without reference to colour, culture or age.

I would make it my concern to engineer a meeting with Mr Curtis, I decided. Just as I wanted to build a dam for myself, so I wanted to establish him as a solid presence in my sight. The sparing and oblique reference to him by Mrs Rutherford, and Christie's latest babbling, led me to believe that he held the clue to the truth of Jack's disappearance. The mystery of Jack would at least give me *something* to engage with until my time came to return to Guyana. Perhaps that was all that was left of England – a faint sense of mystery, enough to twitch your nose; a damp and musty smell, like the books lining the shelves of Mrs Rutherford's cottage. The books told fresh, triumphant stories about the latest deeds of Empire. They spoke with assurance about discoveries in science and manufacturing, about geographical explorations, about the moral conquest of dark and heathen minds. They were certain of the destiny of the English race. But, as Christie rightly said, the Empire had ended and what was left was palsied decay, like the state of the cliff.

I approached Mr Curtis's house, which lay no more than thirty feet from the crumbling cliff's edge. The next collapse was only a matter of time and the house would tumble into the sea. A wall of thickly planted shrubs and tall trees screened the back of the house from prying eyes. I would have to climb one of the trees to get a closer look. There was no one on the path so I pushed against the wall, trying to find a space to poke my head through, without success. I could easily go round to the front of the house, unlock the gate and knock on the door, but how would I introduce myself and what would I then ask of him? I withdrew, but the path was wet and I slipped on an exposed stone, falling untidily into a patch of nettles. I raised my head and panicked, only to be scratched about my eyes and cheeks.

Mrs Rutherford gave me a bowl of hot water to bathe my face, which within a few minutes had swollen alarmingly. 'You look dreadful,' she sympathised, handing me a steaming towel, 'whatever could have happened to you?' She rifled through her medicine cupboard and poured two drops of a black liquid into the bowl. 'That will ease the hurt in no time at all,' she assured me.

'What is it?' I asked, put off by its rank smell.

'Oh just a potion I brewed myself. Stop complaining like a child and do as I say.' She smiled playfully at me as I dabbed the liquid to my eyes. 'You've nearly ruined your trousers as well. It'll be a challenge getting the stains out.' She was glad, it seemed, for the opportunity to fuss over me, and I knew she would apply herself to my clothing in a fresh burst of enthusiasm.

'I slipped and fell over by Mr Curtis's house,' I said, looking for a reaction in her face.

She merely continued brushing the stains from my trousers. 'The path can be treacherous after a downpour of rain, just be careful next time. What shoes are you wearing?' I lifted my foot towards her. 'I'll have to get you a pair with a more secure grip. I'm surprised you've not tumbled over the cliff and broken your neck yet, what with those smooth soles. How's your face doing? Take the towel away, let me have a look.'

'I was trying to peep into his back garden,' I said, hoping to draw her out.

'It's better already, don't you feel so?' She went off and brought a mirror, holding it up before me. 'Just think what Christie will say tomorrow when he sees your eyes all scratched,' she chuckled. 'He'll say we fought and you got the worst of it. You know how he sees me as an overbearing and frustrated woman. Has he been filling your head with more horror stories about me? I bet he didn't tell you the one when I whacked his head so hard that I drew blood and the blow must have resounded through the village?'

'No,' I said, lifting the towel from my face in surprise.

'That's the last time he was invited to work in my garden, I'll tell you,' she said, relishing the memory of her deed. 'Never mind, he didn't mean harm, he's a good sort really. A bit of a coward that's all. He could stand up to Jack but he was appalled by me. You should have seen his hand tremble when I gave him his cup of tea! He spilt half of it in his saucer. I like a man who can look a woman in the eye and declare his desire boldly. If Christie had done so I would have slapped him politely, out of honour, being a married woman and all that. But he fumbled unexpectedly for my mouth and out of fright I laid into him. Poor thing! He dropped his saucer, trowel, packets of herb seeds, the lot, and ran.' She clutched her mouth to contain the mirth. The agedness fled from her body and she became a girl again, shaking with laughter. The mirror fell from her hand and broke into several pieces but the accident only aroused a fresh wave of mirth. I looked at her foolishly through swollen eyes, unable to participate in her mood, for it was provoked by memories too private and intimate. The sight of my piteous condition drove her into hysteria; she pressed her hand to her stomach in pain and retreated upstairs to her room.

'You do loosen and rattle my dentures,' she said, on the verge of more laughter, 'I better go for a jog and wear myself down to my original state.' She had put on her tracksuit and running shoes. 'Next time you want information about Mr Curtis ask me straight, don't fluff about like Christie. Look what it got him – a bloody face. And you, a pair of puffed-up eyes.'

'I wasn't particularly curious about Mr Curtis,' I replied, perplexed by her sudden offer to talk about him when before she had scrupulously avoided the topic. 'It's just that Professor Fenwick, then Christie, suggested that I meet him.'

'Now now, young man,' she said in mock admonishment, 'don't be a coward and go blaming Christie for your error. The two of you are a right pair!' She held up a key to me. 'Take this and unlock the bottom drawer of the desk in my study, you'll find what you've been looking for ever since you set foot in this house.' When I hesitated she pressed the key into my hand. 'Come on Jack,' she called after the dog, 'where are you? Come with Mummy for your walkies.' Jack rushed from his lair in the kitchen and danced about her feet. I watched them through the sitting-room window. Jack bolted ahead at break-neck speed while Mrs Rutherford jogged behind in a painful action, so slow that she seemed to be rooted in one spot.

When she eventually turned the corner and disappeared from sight I went to her study to try the key. There were two albums in the drawer, one containing photographs, the other a collection of newspaper clippings and other items relating to the cliffs. Her history was contained in them, but only in a piecemeal fashion. There were few images of her childhood and only the odd one of her parents. Over the months she had made very little mention of them, always changing the conversation deftly when I tried to probe into her origins. I had only a haphazard sense of her family. She grew up in Nuneaton, a village in the Midlands, an only child who was sent off at an early age to boarding-school. Her father was a dedicated well-to-do tradesman, the maker of fine furniture for the local gentry, and her mother kept the accounts for the business. I could only guess at some unhappiness in her child-hood which made her reluctant to speak of it – loneliness at her boarding-school perhaps, which deepened when she returned during the holidays to a household more accustomed to her absence. Her parents might have greeted her appearance as an intrusion into the routine calmness of their lives, an uncomfort-able reminder of a romantic passion which once promised to be endless, but then waned gradually and was replaced by tolerance, domestic comfort and the business of making a living. Whatever tensions or bitterness erupted to make her shut her parents off from her mind were not exposed by the photographs. They showed neutral images, in fading grey tones, of a child being fed ice-cream or being pushed in a pram along a country lane. Her life began, it seemed, when she met Jack, for most of the photographs were of him, including some of their wedding. She beamed at the camera, gorgeous in her white dress and clutching bouquets of flowers. The guests showered petals over her young face, she laughed like a child, trying to catch as many of them as she could before they fluttered to the ground. She scooped them up and flung them in the air again. The bridesmaids tossed streamers over her. I could easily imagine how her childlike beauty made her a ravishing sight to Jack and with what relish he anticipated the nights of their honeymoon. He looked at the camera stiffly, an ill-concealed nervousness on his face, bordering on guilt. He was tight-lipped, smiling thinly as he struggled to restrain his feelings. The suit seemed ill-fitting, making him fidgety. Yet there was a meekness about him in other photographs, the image of a gentleman who could not conceive of harming his bride in any way. And he was handsome, exceptionally so, and she knew it, for she was unabashed in her delight in being with him. The only disquieting detail was the way he froze before the camera and the crowds, bottling up his true self.

There were no photographs of the honeymoon, as if it were a non-event, another incident she wanted to excise from memory. The rapture of the wedding gave way to images of a common existence. The photographs were cold because there was nothing to convey. She stood in the doorway of a shop. She sat in a pavement café eating cherries. She boarded an aeroplane. She picnicked in a park. They were rarely pictured together and when they were they never looked simultaneously at the camera. She was uncorking the wine while he posed for the photographs; she was paying for candy while he stared at the sea. There was no unison in their lives. The promise that lit up her eyes in the wedding photographs had disappeared utterly, she looked gaunt and prematurely worn. Christie had said Jack was a jealous man, hawkish in his protectiveness towards her, but the images before me suggested frustration, or else a nervous desire to break from the relationship. What frustrations or cruelties had brought them to this state of separation eluded the gaze of the camera. They were so alienated from each other that they became as invisible to each other as I was in the village.

Mr Curtis however appeared on the scene with meteoric splendour. For months all attention was focused on him, his picture appeared regularly in the local newspaper with detailed accounts of his campaign to save the cliffs. This second folder was extremely thick with clippings, pamphlets and other documentation, all of which were deliberately ordered in chronological sequence to enable one to plot the story of Mr Curtis and the cliff. I was intrigued by the care with which Mrs Rutherford had accumulated and ordered the reportage, as if she had been tending a garden. I wondered whether she had been desperately anxious to make sense of events so as to justify an aspect of her personal history. My calculations had hardly begun when I heard the front door rattling. Hurriedly I shoved the folders back into the drawer and made my way into the sitting-room. She came in and went straight to the drinks cabinet, pouring out a large glass of damson wine. She drank it in noisy gulps and then sagged into the sofa to recover her breath. The jog had drained her totally.

'Fetch me another, please,' she asked, holding up her glass feebly. I took it and poured out some wine. 'To the brim, to the brim,' she urged as I dawdled, 'and get yourself one. Come and sit, you make me tired just by looking at you standing up.'

'You should take it easy,' I advised, worried by her exhausted state.

'At my age what's the point? I don't want to unravel and fade away. I'll go in one shriek like a hare being ripped in two. Give me a good run of blood and decanter of wine any day.' She kicked off her plimsolls and wriggled her toes to banish the numbness of her feet. 'I once had silken toes you know,' she said, pointing them coquettishly in my direction, 'but look how crumpled they've become! That's growing old for you. What are your toes like; go on, take off your shoes, let's have a peep.' The run may have drained her strength but it had also made her mentally buoyant and mischievous. 'Come now, you've been gazing upon my naked soul all evening, it's only fair that I have a look at your bits and pieces.' She sipped at her glass to suppress her desire to laugh. 'I run because it makes me feel young again. I like the sensation of my beating heart, like that of an infatuated teenager. I like brushing through the undergrowth along the path and being scratched about. Does that sound weird to you?'

'No, they say it's good for your health,' I replied in as bland a tone as possible.

'What's good for your health? Do you mean running or romance?'

'I meant running.'

'You sound like Jack,' she said, baiting me further.

'Oh? How is that?' I asked, swallowing the wine calmly.

'Well, he thought I was an alcoholic. Isn't that shocking? He'd crawl home after a session of gin and tonics in the Club, having fumbled up all the black servant girls no doubt, and collapse on the bed with his mouth open. I'd watch him dribbling and snorting all night. And he had the temerity to call me a palm-wine drunkard!'

I looked at the drinks cabinet, noticing how well stocked it was, and realised for the first time that during all my months with her she always had a glass in her hand. 'It was only boredom. I'd spend whole days concocting wine from oranges, plums, mangoes, anything that had ripe skin and juice in it. I couldn't bear to drink English spirits with all those English people, so I made my own. Most of it I gave away or poured down the sink, I didn't have the stomach for it. In any case I couldn't get it quite right – it was mostly too crude. Once I drank half a bottle and spent two days in a semi-coma.' She giggled at the memory of Jack rushing around the bedroom with wet towels and a fan, trying to revive her. 'He was more worried about his reputation than my health. It was acceptable for *him* to behave like an indecent clown, but his wife had to be upright, she could never be seen laid out in horizontal debauchery. Men are such fools sometimes, don't you agree?'

'Sometimes,' I said, thinking of my father.

'So what makes you so smart and civilised then? How come you don't believe you're like all the rest?'

'I'm not all that different...'

'But you could never hurt a woman. You don't have it in you.'

'What makes you say that?'

'Well, I've observed you, haven't I?... Unless of course there is a devilish spirit beneath that halo of yours. Tell me, have you ever hurt a woman?'

'I was in love once and it ended,' I lied.

'Love?' she laughed. 'You were never in love. The only person you've cared for is your mother. Don't think I haven't noticed how diligently you wipe the dust from the photograph frame. It's not right you know, all this desire between parent and child. Children have to grow up and move away, otherwise it becomes unhealthy. Jack was sick in that way…' She paused and thought deeply, as if dwelling sadly on her own childhood and on her state of childlessness.

'Jack was odd, wasn't he?' I ventured, hoping to raise her spirits again, 'didn't you find him sinister?' I expected a moment of agitation in which she would recollect their time together and perhaps fumble for an answer. Instead she replied calmly, as if he was still fresh in her mind even after decades of separation.

'Jack was thoroughly an Englishman,' she said. 'He wore starched collars, and braces held up his trousers, but still he yearned for some kind of slackness or freedom. He didn't know what he wanted but he'd get it nevertheless, by accident or by great cruelty – either physical or mental cruelty or both. He'd achieve freedom but in the process he'd snuff out someone else's. Afterwards he would be sorry and try to make amends, or else he would not be sorry and act more viciously than before to justify the original sin. He was either the backbone of the Empire or the penitent who surrendered the Empire, paid back some of the money and retreated to the island and village of his home. He returned from Africa with me but he couldn't settle. He was restless. He had to go back for more.'

'Christie says he was a feeble sort, suffering from palpitations of the heart.'

'That's odd. I didn't think he had a heart. He was mostly mouth and genitalia. If he was ill it would have been from infected mucous at either end… Still, I shouldn't be so wicked. What's gone is gone for ever, and I did love him once upon a time. I was the one with the heart, you should have heard how loudly and excitedly it used to beat.' She yawned, the wine suddenly making her tipsy and tired. Her hands clamped the arms of the sofa, trying to raise her body, but it was too heavy and she sank deeper into the seat. She looked at me helplessly as if beseeching me to take her to bed but knowing that I would be too inadequate to make the offer.

I stayed up until she fell asleep, then went to fetch a blanket to cover her. She looked frail and pathetic, a ghost of her true self. As I tucked the blanket around her body I thought of Roosevelt slumped over his machine, and of all the ghosts of my past, all those who once beckoned me by the mystery and glamour of their character but who then faded and disappeared when I approached too closely.

TEN

The next day Mrs Rutherford gave me complete access to the Curtis file, putting it herself in my briefcase before sending me off to work. 'Something to entertain you in your tea-break,' she said, as if it were some pulp novel.

For the next two weeks my tea-breaks were unexpectedly lengthy, for there was little work to do. A series of accidents interrupted the construction of the sea-wall. Firstly, the main crane which lifted the heaviest boulders into place kept slipping its tracks and threatening to collapse in a murderous heap of metal. Then Mr Rushton, on one of his rare excursions out of his hut on to the working area of the beach, slipped on a rock and twisted his ankle. His calculating finger was intact but the damage to his foot was too painful on the brain so he took time off. Mr Rushton's misfortune was soon visited upon several other workmen. As soon as he disappeared a rash of accidents and illnesses prevented them clocking on for days. Christie claimed to have fractured his arm when he slipped and fell heavily against a boulder. The beach had suddenly become dangerous, as if some wicked spirit or leprechaun had coated each pebble and stone with invisible grease. Three or four men claimed to have toppled and sprained this or that part of their anatomy. A virus which brought on giddiness and lethargy affected a few others, and they too reported sick. Of course it was not my business to comment on the various mishaps or to seek alternative temporary workers. I had no authority over them, for I was only an adjunct to Professor Fenwick, a junior engineer whose role was to advise on the technical aspects of the project. Mr Rushton and a handful of lieutenants were in charge, and since they were off sick there was nothing to do but gaze out of the cabin and await their return. Meanwhile the cracks that had opened up in the cliff grew wider. Water, reddened by ores embedded in the rocks, trickled out between the cracks, staining the white face of the cliff. It looked painfully wounded, the victim of some gross abuse. Great cavities disfigured its face, like eye-sockets from which flesh and membrane had been sucked out. Various serrations, also the aftermath of previous collapses, added to its appearance of abuse. The wind and the sea continued to finger it, and I was helpless to offer protection.

The hut became my retreat from this disorder and the fate of Mr Curtis my only deliberation. I read and re-read the file, constructing his story partly from my own speculations, partly from the newspaper items, but mostly from a lengthy pamphlet which a supporter and admirer of Mr Curtis had penned to justify the chronicle of his actions to the world. It was written in such a lofty style that it was obviously addressed to an audience bigger than the few hundred people of the village. The style also suggested an audience of the future rather than a purely immediate and temporary one.

From ordinary beginnings the issue of the cliffs catapulted him into the limelight. He was in his late forties, a quiet bachelor who worked for a firm of stockbrokers in the City and who came home at weekends to his cottage. *He loved nothing more than tramping village lanes and wooded paths, an intense and solitary man barely known to his neighbours,* the pamphlet had it, painting a romantic portrait of genius, preparing us for his inevitable downfall. He lavished all his money on his cottage, constantly renovating and repainting it. *More often than not he would be seen on a Saturday afternoon perched on the roof, removing bird droppings and dead leaves from the gutters or banging nails, struggling against high winds which threatened to topple him.* (Many such banal details were naïvely dropped into a narrative of otherwise high purpose.) The villagers viewed him as a typical city man enchanted by the freedoms that the countryside offered. They tolerated him, for his obsessions were harmless enough, until one weekday when twenty feet of cliff crashed upon the beach. He was devastated when he came home that

129

Friday. He stayed indoors all weekend, brooding. His garden had shrunk to three-fifths of its original size and it was clear that the next collapse would bring the house so close to the brink that it would become uninhabitable. *After a weekend of grief and panic he dreamt up a scheme which seized the attention of the whole village. He abandoned his job to dedicate his middle-age to saving his house.*

Four huge trucks rumbled through the village early one morning and parked outside Mr Curtis's house. Before long a few villagers gathered out of curiosity as the workmen began unloading scaffolding, jacks and all kinds of heavy equipment. The photographer from the local newspaper captured Mr Curtis greeting the local workmen. *He looked rugged and obsessed as he showed them the spot in the front garden where new foundations were to be established.* There was no time to lose and under his stern and tight-lipped direction they began digging to a depth of six feet and a length and width of fifty yards. All day wheelbarrows of earth were tipped over the cliff edge. It was slow work and the onlookers came and went in shifts. Some, captivated by the energy and riskiness of the venture, volunteered their services, bringing pots of tea to the workmen, offering advice or helping to erect poles or brick pediments. Soon there was a spirit of carnival over the whole village. Mr Curtis had suddenly injected excitement into their lives and they rallied to him with their garden spades, rakes, and any tool that came to hand which could break and disperse earth. *He had in one imaginative act destroyed the inertia of the place.* For decades the land was slowly disappearing as storms loosened and toppled segments of cliff. They had done nothing but watch house after house crash on to the beach like so many shipwrecked arks. Now Mr Curtis was braving the sea as no one in living memory had done, and at stupendous personal expense. To move the house thirty-five feet inland would easily cost him £20,000. That a stranger to the village was willing to invest such a sum intrigued them. They felt ashamed of their own meanness of spirit and inactivity.

It took two days for the foundations to be prepared and the house underpinned and supported on a steel frame. Another day was spent moving the whole structure over scaffolding poles, inch by inch, on jacks. Admiration for Mr Curtis grew by the

130

hour, so that when the house was eventually rolled back and settled he had become a man of enormous stature, no longer the eccentric city gent slipping about a rural roof-top.

Inspired by the adulation of the village, he launched another do-it-yourself project, more daring than the earlier one: an attempt no less to build his own sea-defence to protect his portion of the cliff. A dredger, a crane and a bulldozer made deep holes in the sand, lifted metal poles – lumps of disused railway sleepers – and inserted them into the holes. Hundreds of old car tyres filled with grit and concrete were then dropped upon the poles. This wall of steel and rubber was designed to protect the toe of the cliff directly below his portion of land. The scheme was simplicity itself compared with the engineering feats most villagers assumed were needed to save the cliffs. The wall held for a few days, breaking and diminishing the power of the waves, and Mr Curtis's reputation soared, until a malicious tide shifted some poles sideways and some tyres floated off. When the tide subsided, old tyres and debris littered the coastline for miles eastward. *A few villagers spoke against Mr Curtis, in muted tones, but like all cowards they managed to insinuate their complaints into the ear of the Council's environment officer.* He duly arrived at the beach to investigate, and immediately issued an order for the removal of the wall, which had been erected without planning permission. Mr Curtis's house had also been moved illegally, but seeing that it would be an impossible engineering feat to push it uphill back to its original spot, a curt letter was issued warning him against future breaches of Council regulations.

The threat of Council interference roused him into action. Years of accountancy-training had bred a certain reasonableness in him which was now ripped away. The mild-mannered man plunged into a rage which changed the course of the village's history and endowed him with a lasting reputation as monster or saviour, depending on which side one took. He called a public meeting in the Church Hall, nailing handwritten posters on prominent trees and dropping leaflets through doors. A downpour of rain loosened and smudged his posters, but people pitied his misfortune and braved the weather to turn up in large numbers. He began meekly enough, coughing occasionally to clear the nervousness in his throat. He fumbled with his sentences. As time went on however and he sensed the sympathy of the crowd, his neck stiffened. He looked directly in their midst and became more fluent. *He brushed aside the microphone, addressing them in a naked, passionate voice.* He outlined a history of the surrounding countryside they barely knew and certainly didn't expect to hear from the mouth of a stranger. The place was always threatened by foreign invasions, he told them, barbarians from Europe who laid waste to the villages in acts of unimaginable sadism. *Every endeavour was smashed before it could take root, history was a trail of discontinuities. The savages were aided and abetted by English collaborators, the enemy within who were as heinous as the outsiders. They consisted of high-ranking and lesser officials, all those who controlled taxes and existed on the labour of others. They collaborated with the invaders to protect their privileges, to regulate the processes of theft.* Even now, he argued, officials representing the District Council were bare-faced in their scorn for the populace. They were allowing Dunsmere to disintegrate, refusing to spend a penny on sea-defence. They were lining their own pockets with taxpayers' money, renovating their meeting-places with chandeliers and plush furniture. Or else they wasted time debating the quantity of dung lying in the sands, appointing dog wardens to patrol the beaches in the tourist season. They passed laws relating to the noise of lawnmowers or the height of hedges, unconcerned by the disappearance of the gardens. What was needed was concerted protest by ordinary folk, for it was their action that, historically, curbed official excesses.

The villagers clapped uncomfortably, acknowledging the eloquence of his address yet resentful that they should be classed as commoners and underdogs. They were also fearful of his call to arms: their lives were settled and the only disruption to the place in recent memory was the lorryloads of machinery brought in by Mr Curtis himself. Perhaps the Council was right, perhaps he was a troublemaker wanting to disturb the tranquil order of the village that their forefathers had fought to establish against foreign and city invaders. The sea was part of the rhythm of their lives, and they had grown accustomed to the erosion of land. What was the loss of a few houses and a hundred feet of cliffs a year, but an honourable tribute to a sea that had given them their livelihood as sailors, fishermen, innkeepers? In any case a stable bay would eventually form, the sea would cease exacting tribute and a new trickle of sightseers would replenish the wealth of the district.

When the meeting dispersed only a handful of the villagers agreed with his proposal to set up a Committee for the Defence of Dunsmere, and they consisted entirely of the occupants of the twelve or thirteen houses under immediate threat. The newspaper's photograph showed them all to be women. He looked very much like a master among disciples, the camera capturing the protective way in which they flanked him, jostling for the closest position, eyeing him nervously, whilst he stared out above their heads to some greater but as yet unseen destiny.

They disappeared from the subsequent coverage, which focused entirely on his individual efforts. *He went about giving talks to sympathetic local societies, then widened his appeal in a swathe of rhetoric spreading from Dunsmere to the heart of London.* One photograph showed him outside the House of Commons shaking hands with a group of politicians. Another pictured him holding up a letter he had written to the Queen Mother. There were accounts of his work in the national journals, and although they were small items swallowed up in a sea of newsprint, they revealed his remarkable progress as an orator and campaigner. His utterances were grander than his coverage: *he spoke of courage, of the soul of the nation that had survived two world wars and triumphed over tyranny, and of the corruption of virtue by unpatriotic bureaucrats and time-servers.* His rhetoric, wedded to his single-mindedness, suggested that he could have easily been the leader of an extreme party in different circumstances and with a greater cause than cliff erosion. There was nothing extreme about his followers though, the housewives and widows galvanised into fund-raising through garden fêtes, tombolas and car-boot sales. They went about their tasks not with fervour but more in a naïve discovery of self-worth. They suddenly had important roles to play, whether tramping through fields and valleys on sponsored walks or devising patterns to make leaflets bearing Mr Curtis's exhortations more attractive to the eye. The folder contained cards they had designed bearing touching if homespun verse which they sold to tourists' shops in the district; verse lamenting not so much the loss of the cliffs but the romance of their own lives:

Sit here upon this precipice
Bathed in the moon's light which one day
Will not see the bliss
Nor the heart's play.
The cliffs erode and fall away
Into death's abyss.

Such dirges were illustrated by drawings of solitary figures standing at the edge of the cliff, ankle-deep in night-mist which threatened to erase them. Mr Curtis had provoked them into ardent poetry of a sort, and a sense of their mortality.

At the end of the first month the Defence Committee had enjoyed themselves and amused the villagers by their antics but had achieved nothing. Mr Curtis's fiery speeches continued, and the women arranged more fairs, but no one paid much attention to the cause, until, four months into the campaign, a letter from the Queen Mother arrived. Mr Curtis summoned the Committee and the local photographer to his drawing-room, the campaign headquarters. *There was an air of sacred drama as he opened the envelope with his paper-knife, making sure not to damage the letter.* Gently he eased it out. He paused in respect before beginning to read it aloud. It was jubilant news but he maintained a reverent voice to the end. Only then did he allow a smile to flash across his face. The women broke into applause and swarmed around him, caught between wanting to hold the letter and to hold him. The Queen Mother had given her blessing to their efforts to preserve the nation's heritage represented in its farmlands and cliffs. She would watch events unfurl with interest. In the mean time she was passing their letter on to the Ministry of Agriculture and to the Directors of the National Trust.

When the news broke throughout the district the Council called an emergency meeting. Grim-faced officials faced the national press to explain their inactivity over the years. It would take millions of pounds, they explained, to build adequate sea-defences, and the cost to the rate payer would be devastating, necessitating a hike in local rates of at least sixpence in the pound. Coastal protection was more properly the business of central government, but in deference to the Queen Mother they would immediately commission a Sensitivity Analysis and Technical Appraisal. They would reconvene within three months to consider what action to take in the light of information received. Twelve thousand pounds would be allocated to engage the services of a team of consultants. In the mean time the nation was to be assured of the Council's deep regard for the Royal Family and for the recreational and the aesthetic value of Dunsmere Cliff, and the Council would do everything in its power to preserve it.

Their bland pronouncements however only sharpened Mr Curtis's appetite for action. *He called a celebratory sherry party, rallying the spirits of his band of followers, inciting them to hound the Council to the point of exhaustion and meek surrender.* Mrs Rutherford had turned up to that party, partly out of curiosity and partly because her house was one of those threatened by cliff erosion. As Mr Curtis spoke he must have looked into the faces of the women and realised the hopelessness of the campaign ahead. They would organise coffee mornings, barbecues, auctions and other genteel fund-raising drives, but what was needed now was tactical assaults upon the District Council by way of carefully worked-out strategies of protest and manipulation of information. He needed a supportive intellect to spearhead the campaign, a fellow-conspirator. As his eyes alighted on Mrs Rutherford he must have sensed her difference from the rest of the flighty and excitable women. She was standing apart from them, sipping her sherry quietly, maintaining a superior distance from their chattering. He must have gone up to her and recruited her there and then, but neither the pamphlet nor the clippings revealed how she was seduced into his fold.

She began to appear in the newspapers, initially through sparse references to her name but eventually in photographs of the two of them heading a picket outside the Town Hall or handing in a petition to the Ministry of Agriculture. It was obvious that she added glamour to the campaign, complementing his sombre speech-making. Even the monochrome reproductions could not dampen the energy of her presence. She looked as sensuous and alert as she did in the earlier wedding photographs. Mr Curtis had brought her back to life but she was purposeful and intelligent, not flirtatious like the other women. (The pamphlet contained such privileged access to personal information, and depicted Mrs Rutherford so vividly, that I began to suspect that she was its author.) It was she who pored over the Council's proposals for sea-defences, deeming them to be cheap and flimsy constructions. She wrote criticism of them in a series of technical notes to Mr Curtis. He embroidered them with colourful adjectives, stood up at Council meetings and thundered forth objections. *He poured scorn on their gabionade, groynes and tadpole headlands, calling for a more monumental feat of engineering which would be the glory of England's south and the wonder of Europe. He pointed to the Aswan Dam and other mighty and marvellous constructions in lesser countries: the Council's counterfeit defences would not reinforce the cliffs, they would only reinforce the world's dangerous opinion that England was a nation in decline.* The supporters clapped at his rhetoric, but the substance of his speech was of Mrs Rutherford's making. She sat composed in the Council Chamber's gallery, secretly delighted by the success of the long nights she had spent flicking through complex scientific proposals put forward by the consultants. She had no previous training, but managed somehow to decipher the jargon with nothing more than the aid of the *Oxford English Dictionary*. Whilst she had no hard evidence of the technical inadequacy of the Council's proposals, her inbuilt distrust of officialdom sustained her attacks on them.

The battle over the cliffs dragged on for years, the balance of power see-sawing between the Council and the Defence Committee. The pressure of the attacks and counter-attacks plunged the village into a state bordering on civil war. The majority of villagers, fearful of a steep rise in the local rates, resented Mr Curtis and his band, who in turn accused them of selfishness. They cared nothing for the integrity of the land, the Defence Committee argued, because their portions of it were sufficiently far from the cliffs not to be jeopardised in the short term. In fifty years' time however the sea would swallow up their houses, so they were uncaring too of the future of their children's inheritance. Such disintegration of family values was mirrored in the state of the cliff. The abandonment of responsibility to family exemplified the disgraceful state of the nation as a whole. Our Victorian ancestors would be shocked by our loss of values. *We once gathered the world in a commonwealth of nations, bringing harmony where there was discord, seeding and nurturing civilised ideas in the most far-flung moral wastelands. Now we were in veritable collapse, each sickly man for himself.*

The majority of the villagers resented Mr Curtis's condemnations, they deemed him arrogant and his sea-defence schemes grandiose. They remembered the recent war, the monstrous egoism of Mussolini and Hitler, and they shrank from him. Rumours began to circulate, which the newspapers picked up on (the pamphlet was silent at this point), that Mr Curtis was in fact a second-generation immigrant who had Anglicised his name so as to disappear into the crowd. His attitude though could not hide his foreignness. The Queen Mother's support of him was also dubious. 'After all, the Windsors were of German stock and they have married Greeks, and worse,' one villager was quoted as saying to a journalist. Some of the villagers moved from being Royalists by instinct to a scandalous and confused Republicanism. Most of them longed for the peace of bygone days, when they could walk their dogs along the cliff-top, or picnic with friends and family, secure in the feeling of good-neighbourliness and the common decencies which bound one to another. Mr Curtis retaliated by calling them counterfeit and nostalgic. *The germs of the demise of the Empire lay in their cowardice.* Where was the robustness, he asked, shown on the beaches of Normandy, where was the sacrifice made at the battle of Isandhlwana?

In a previous stage of evolution they would have swung axes at each other's heads or set up ambushes along the cliff-top. The blood-letting would have been as ready as any tribal feud in the Congo. Now however they established rival committees, sent venomous messages and memoranda, passed passionate resolutions and refused to nod to each other as they queued up for their pensions at the post office. They leant over fences or met in shaded places to gossip, stopping abruptly when someone else passed whose politics they were unsure of; their eyes followed the intruder until he disappeared from sight before they resumed their plotting. The Association of Citizens (AC), the gang opposed to the Defence Committee (DC), became the source of infectious rumours which travelled in whispers but as effectively as any messages beaten out on an African drum. The principal smear inevitably concerned an affair between Mr Curtis and Mrs Rutherford. On their various trips to London to lobby politicians, it was said that they frequently sojourned in hotels around Waterloo before boarding the train back to Dunsmere. The moral welfare of the village children was threatened by this woman's liaison with Mr Curtis, it was alleged, for her husband Jack was a governor of one of the district primary schools. A petition bearing eighty-three names was raised in an attempt to remove him from his position, even though he seemed to have taken no part in the campaign.

The cuttings ended abruptly on this whiff of scandal; I rummaged about the folder to pick up the trail but there was nothing else. (The pamphlet had ended on a more triumphant note, quoting from a letter sent by a Member of Parliament to the Prime Minister, recommending Mr Curtis for an OBE.) Was this all England had to offer me – a seedy narrative of adultery and civic squabbles? I was more than ever confused by the snapshots and piecemeal composition of the lives of these English villagers. I thumbed through the articles again, wanting to read between the lines to discover the fuller story of Mrs Rutherford's attachment to Mr Curtis. How *could* she have given support and solace to a man of such dangerously patriotic sentiments? Was she previously as conservative as he was? Did Jack remove her to a foreign place to escape the shame of their affair? Did he beat her, as Christie alleged? Did the encounter with Africa clarify her views about England in a blinding illumination, as its masks had suddenly benighted me? Was her enlightenment juxtaposed to my own sense of darkness, the masks working a grotesque and ironic magic which propelled her into the future and me into the past? As usual there was only a series of questions left with me, each revelation bearing its distorted shadow.

For two weeks I surveyed the materials, calculating the story with the intelligence of an engineer. Mrs Rutherford was stubbornly reticent all this time, refusing to talk about anything but cliff-defence. The more I insinuated Mr Curtis's name into our tea-time conversations, the more she pressed me on the progress of the sea-dam, as if it had become a symbol of her desire to keep me at bay. She even took to curtailing our talks by switching on the television, claiming she wanted to follow some soap. Sullenly I watched the actors playing out elaborate and unreal lives. 'I read in the papers they're due to kill off Barrington-Moore,' she said at the end of the show: 'Shame. He's such a handsome young thing. I dare say they'll resurrect him in some shape or form in future episodes though. That's the way these soaps work.' I knew she was only affecting interest in the absurd television drama to frustrate my real questions.

'I'm fed up with reportage,' I blurted out after sitting through one such episode and listening to her babble on about what would happen next week.

'Reportage? That's a fancy word for a soap programme isn't it? It's only a bit of harmless fun. Relax.' I was in no mood for relaxing though. She had given me the folder, provoked my appetite for more, then coolly withdrawn her favours.

'I'm just fed up with second-hand information, what I see on television or read in the papers. There must be more to this place, some reality or other…'

'You still want to connect, is that it?' she asked, a hint of amusement in her eyes.

'Of course I want to connect… with something real and solid.'

'You mean something fleshy?'

'If you like. Yes, something fleshy… even if it stinks,' I added, thinking of Christie's description of fulsome English bodies.

'Why should it be malodorous?' she asked, putting it more elegantly so as to becalm my brutal mood.

'I don't care. So long as it exists. I'm beginning to think nothing exists in England. Everything is a reported story. You can't know anything for certain. Take Jack. There's not a trace of him here, yet we keep mentioning his name. Take Curtis. He's a photo-graph in a newspaper and a lot of descriptions, that's all. As to the villagers, I've rarely seen any of them in real life. They might as well be Christie's ghosts.'

139

'But they are ghosts. There's only me and you and the sea-wall left, the only concrete certainties. Everything else has gone. Why not accept that?' She put the question to me with such force that I sensed that she was addressing herself.

'How do you mean "gone"?' I asked, my probing growing gentler so as not to evoke hurt in her.

'Gone, that's all, departed, excised, evaporated, absconded, whatever word you want to use. Even you had disappeared before you showed up here. You had lost yourself in your computations so as to disguise all the traces of your African past, but these masks brought you face to face with yourself. That's why they still set you on edge. You're on edge, like the faults in the cliff, one stratum grating against the next, the whole lot threatening to topple because of the tension. I watch you watching the masks in silence, but I can hear all the grating noises of your thoughts. Just relax, that's all.'

'I can't relax when you've given me pieces of a story to read but wouldn't tell me what the whole of it is,' I retaliated. 'What's the point of constructing the whole of a sea-wall? Why don't I build it just partially?'

'Relax,' she insisted, 'I want you to *know* the whole story. But perhaps I should keep you on edge. Perhaps that's why you are driven, because you're always on edge, either between your mother and a lover or…'

'Swami once said that to me,' I interrupted, partly to prevent her dwelling on my sexuality, partly because Swami had been haunting me of late. Now that the sea-wall was nearing completion I kept recalling his warnings. 'One of my workers in Guyana,' I explained. 'He told me I lived at the edge of a ruler, afraid to venture off in case I collapsed in a heap of madness. He was wrong. It was he who disintegrated. I'll build the sea-wall and the cliff *will* be saved.'

'You sound like Curtis, don't you think?' she said in a devastating tone of voice. I was suddenly and overwhelmingly blinded by the comparison, as if she had directed a floodlight into my eye.

'Why do you keep a garden, then? If you don't believe in a certain order, why do you maintain your garden as you have maintained Curtis's folder?'

140

'You are not Curtis,' she said, as if to pacify me. 'For all his straight talk he was crooked and a fraud. He was dreaming cruel deeds all the time, like Jack. You don't have that layer of cruelty in you. That's why I've kept the garden, I suppose, to remind me of their Englishness, their cruelty. It's the most English thing I can do. As you say, it's all order on the surface. I kept it that way for years so that one day somebody like you would come from far away and disturb it. Like the reverse of an English fairy tale, where the white knight arrives to restore order and security to the imprisoned maiden. I wanted an African to arrive and disrupt the place, perhaps one of the children I used to teach so long ago, a devil in the garden. Before you showed up all I had were my spiteful masks. But you disappointed all my dreams.'

'I came to protect your house and to protect you,' I said, wanting in turn to console her even though my words sounded as foolish as any in a fairy tale.

'I didn't need protection. I needed to be scandalised. I needed you to tell me what I was in the cruellest language of your tribe. That's why I gave you the folder and left you alone with it, refusing to speak further. You were to have total freedom to make up the story of England, to interpret it with the same abandonment with which we described and dominated your lot. Instead it seems you've been piecing bit by bit, objectively and mechanically, instead of letting your imagination rip! Didn't I tell you before to drop all your engineering methods if you were to find out the real story of England? Didn't I?' She stared at me as if daring me to victimise her, but knowing that I would disappoint her, that I was not cruel enough to cause havoc. But it was not because I was a mere engineer, occupied with building and restoring, that prevented me from retaliating against her 'Englishness'. Even though she offered herself to me as a victim she knew all along that my peculiar and deviant love for her would banish any such urge to destruction. I could no more accuse her than I could accuse my mother of sleeping with the preacherman, though the evidence of both their sinning was obvious to an engineer trained to interpret data objectively.

ELEVEN

'Sure he's dying of a broken heart,' Christie said, determined to play the part of an 'Irishman' as stubbornly as Mrs Rutherford in her garden pretended to be an 'Englishwoman'.

'Don't give me that romantic nonsense, man. What's the real truth? When did you last see him, for instance? And what's he up to now?'

'A broken heart I tell you,' Christie insisted, 'it's obvious isn't it? Why else would a bloke like Mr Curtis shut himself away?'

'But do you *know* that for certain or is it your Irish imagination? You seem to put everything down to people with good hearts and bad hearts – you said the same about Jack.' He took offence immediately and I retracted and fumbled for an apology. 'What I mean is that you tend to put things in the best possible light. You have a way of livening up situations…'

'You mean I'm a bloody liar don't you?'

'No I didn't say that, that's unfair. I wouldn't be sitting in a man's house enjoying his hospitality and insulting him at the same time, what do you take me for?' As if to prove the point I finished the cup of tea he had made, poured myself another and bit hard into a fresh biscuit.

He poked about the fire and fed it more wood. 'Well you're spot-on at that, I am a downright honest liar,' he said, turning round and waving the poker in my direction, 'and a good thing too. If only you knew!' He put down the poker as if to free his hands for more conciliatory gestures. 'Look,' he said pointing to the ramshackle shelves bearing chipped crockery, to the dining-table with its stained surface, and the sprinkling of soft chairs all leaking foam. 'I could tell you I had better days but you'd think

I'd be lying. What would Christie know about wealth, you'd ask yourself, what would he know about pâté in an ornamental dish or scoops of foie gras and that? How can Christie handle a fish-knife you may ask, would he know which way the curve at the top should be turned before he cuts into his cod? Come now, tell the truth.'

'I never judge anyone by their appearance and present circumstances,' I said, hoping to sound as plausible and philosophic as possible given the obvious shambles of the house, which seemed to reflect a trait in his character.

He pounced on me. 'That's a lie for a start and a right royal one. But then I forget that you are royalty, the prince of your tribe, what with your face all polished like mahogany. Sure I've upset you now, you're shifting uneasy in your pants, you think I'm a bigot and you want to leap up and clout me for calling you black. But you're too royal for a fist-fight, aren't you?'

'I'm no different from you, Christie, so why should I want to antagonise you?' I asked, hoping to calm him down.

He wouldn't respond to my effort at peace-making though. He seemed to want to work himself into a rage. My presence seemed to make him want to confess all kinds of submerged truths. 'It's not you,' he said, sensing my feeling of injury, 'it's them,' and he waved his hand at the door as if dismissing crowds congregated there. 'To me you're different, you're as foreign as them…' His passion subsided for a moment while he considered what he had just uttered. 'You're… you're… you know,' he stammered, struggling to pinpoint what it was that moved him to bouts of anger, 'I just detest the bastards. I've lived so long among them that I've become one of them. They have everything and they have the words and all. You're one of them too, it's only you're wearing a face of mahogany. You're them but you're different from them and I'm all confused. What the hell are you? Why did you come to my house?'

'Because you invited me,' I said, watching his face bubble with inexplicable hatred.

'No one comes to my house. I live here alone. It's at the edge of the village and there's no path, you have to beat through bush to get to me. So why are you here, how did you find the place?'

'I followed the line of poplars as you said and took the turnings you drew on this paper.' I fished out his hand-drawn map and gave it to him.

'You miss the point!' he said, taking the paper, screwing it up and throwing it into the fire. 'What I mean is, what do you want coming here? Not to see me, that's for sure, and you couldn't have been interested in the house. It's crooked-backed and leaning, you must have seen thousands of buildings like this in your own country, so what's new?' He looked sourly at me, taunting me to rise to his insults, but I kept my composure.

'I'll go if you like.'

'Do as you please.' He walked away to the fireplace and poked about violently, giving vent to his passion. He went outside and I could hear him hacking impotently at a log, wanting to reduce it to pieces of wood which he would further reduce to ash. He returned to chuck a handful into the fire, watching the flames suck out the moisture and blister the wood. 'Oh, you're still here,' he said in mock surprise, turning round and gazing upon me. 'Not finished your tea yet, is that it? I might as well behave English-like and join you.' He approached and sat on the sofa opposite me, folding his legs politely and smiling.

'Shall I pour you some?' I asked, going along with his folly, since it was pointless leaving without trying to find out what made him behave so frantically.

'This is what you call Irish hospitality,' he said after a long pause, 'you must have heard what a giving race we are. In our villages in Ireland we feed any stranger who pops into the house until he's bloated, we turn out the children to give him a bed and give the eldest daughter to warm it for him. Go on, have another biscuit.' He shoved them towards me. His hand trembled, the biscuits rattled on the plate and I took the one closest to the brink to save it falling on the floor.

'Look here Christie, I've come all peaceably. You and I have got on in the months we've been working together, haven't we?' I pleaded with him.

'Just about,' he growled.

'Come on now, what have I done to you?'

'You unsettle me. You confuse me with all your questions. You make me nervous. Things were all right before you came, every-thing held down, but you're as devilish as your black face. You speak few words and act all timid but deep down you're a sly one.'

'Come on, Christie, you've made me at home here from the very first day on the beach. You talk to me, you tell me all the gossip of the village. You're my only mate, where would I be without you?' My appeal for his continued friendship softened him. I realised that as long as I played the role of the hapless underdog I could connect with his mood. Not wanting to risk a relapse, I pressed my case. 'I'd be lonely were it not for your chat over the weeks, pining for Guyana as much as you pine for Ireland.'

'Well now, that's a strong word. I know what you're trying to say but I wouldn't go so far as to say *pine*. You pine for your dead wife, for your sister who has emigrated to Boston or Australia, you pine for the job you once held down that paid enough for the flashiest clothes and the flashiest women, that kind of thing, but never for Ireland. Not *Ireland*. Where have you been for the last hundred years? In the bush I suppose.'

'One more insult from you and I'm off,' I said sternly, sensing that I had regained control of his affections.

'Oh, you are touchy today, aren't you?' he chided me.

'What do you expect? I've come all the way here, on my day off, and all I've been getting from you is nigger, nigger, nigger.' The repetition of the word disarmed him totally. A look of shame contorted his face. He fumbled with the teapot.

'I'm a nigger myself,' he mumbled apologetically, his head lowered, too cowardly to look me in the eye. 'The difference between us is that I know all about your place, cannibals and all that, mud and starvation, but you don't know that Ireland is the same. How can you pine for a place that is one big field of potatoes?'

'I've heard that Ireland was all jigs and reels and poetry,' I said teasingly.

'I heard the same but all I knew was potatoes.'

'Are you sure you're not being Irish and feeling sorry for yourself?' I ventured, looking around at the room and wondering whether its desolation was not designed.

145

'"Being" Irish? What's that? For sure, playing Paddy, but "being" Irish is sheer bull. Playing Paddy is our national pastime: I joke, I grin, I talk in a bog accent, I get drunk and slur my grammar, I plot, I wave my shovel at demonstrations against the English, I believe in fairies. I've been playing Paddy so long I've forgotten what it feels like to be a man, never mind an Irishman. After a while you crawl into your own entrails and disappear up your own disguise. No one can find you, not even yourself. I might as well be Jack for all you know. Did you also hear I had a wife that I left?'

'It wouldn't surprise me. All the men I've come across seem to have left their wives.'

'Well, I tell a lie. I never had one but if I did I would have surely left her, being a Paddy and all. Truth is she died on me.' His face quickened with sadness and he grew silent. I stared at my shoes, unsure of how to react. 'Not really,' he said in a sprightly voice and tapped me on the shoulder, 'don't be so morose. The hag picked up and peregrinated with a younger man back to the barley-fields of Galway, or somewhere. That was two decades ago and I've been merry ever since. I've bent or broken every pot, cup and bench in this house in howling celebration. I've slept with every widow, spinster and prowling female in the village, including Mrs Rutherford. You see me haggard now, a man wasted by sloth and sin, on the very brink of perdition. But do I care? Do I look as if I care? Do I care how I look? Oh no, not Christie, not this Paddy, never in a lifetime. That's where I differ from Curtis, you see. Janet was a classic murderess. She strung Curtis along and he hanged himself in grief. She withdrew to the furthest point in primitive Africa, when he was at the very peak of manhood and conquest, just about to win a great victory against his Council enemies. It was to be the dawn of a new civilisation, this sea-dam of his. Talk about cruelty! You should have seen him, poor bastard. He ranted on for a few more weeks, bless him, then fell upon his own small English prick, a martyr to the cause of love. Fuck the English and fuck the tea lad, let's have some whiskey.' He shot upright, swiped the teapot from the table and dumped it in the sink. He fished out a bottle of whiskey from one of the cupboards and plonked it before me. 'I do sometimes. Not often mind you, but just now and again,' he said in a low confessional voice, pouring out a large glass for himself.

'Do what?' I asked, alarmed by his edginess.

'I do care... about all the things I've done or undone. Once in a while only, no point working yourself into a state of promise or distress. Let's drink to a happy burial of the past? No more resurrections, no more rag-and-bone corpses breaking through from deep under to take us by the throat.' He shuddered and drank his whiskey in one go, pouring out another immediately. 'Just imagine all those worms.'

'What about Mr Curtis then?' I asked, trying to shift the conversation away from the morbid.

'A right worm that man was,' he persisted, 'they say he's dying of leprosy. Moths are eating away at his skin as he once ate away at women's sex.'

'I thought you said he was dying of sorrow.'

'That was me I was on about, when the wife left, I mean. Even now. You can easily tell from the way my hand shakes.' He shoved out his hand for me to examine. 'Rushton swears it's liquor, says I can't break stone cleanly any more so he'll sack me. What would that worm know about romance? It's no point even arguing with him. In any case I know a few stories about him that would put him behind bars. I can tell all about how he defrauds the company in shady deals with the suppliers. He's got his hand in the till but one day they'll bang it shut and break all his grubby little fingers. Then there's a man called Fenwick in London that he slips money to, the man who drew up the whole project.'

'Fenwick? You don't mean Professor Fenwick?'

'That's the one, a right brain-box, a college prof I hear he is, and a right crook. Rushton and him have been at it for years, even before the work on the beach began. They had some dirty little secret going to defraud the Council, telling them that they need so many million tons of rock to build a sea-wall when they needed less. The barges arrived and dumped the rocks they ordered, but who's going to weigh each one to find out whether the proper tonnage was delivered? The councillors are too busy with their own dirty little secrets to bother, fiddling their travelling and hospitality expenses, and they haven't got a bathroom scale big enough to do the weighing... Now that there's nothing left in Ireland, the English are stealing from each other. Have a drink, lad, and put some colour back in that black face of yours, you look as if you've seen a ghost.'

'How have you come by all these stories?' I demanded, struggling to restrain my temper.

'There you go again! You never give up do you? Always asking questions. What is Mr Curtis? Where is Mr Curtis? Why is Mr Curtis? Tell me, who is Mr Curtis to you or you to Mr Curtis? Do you think he's tossing in his bed with gonorrhoeal fever right now wondering about you? I keep telling you, don't pry into this country. Keep to yourself. Act black and dumb. Get the banjo out. Sing like Al Jolson. Run the hundred metres at the Olympics. Do anything but don't enquire too deeply or you're done for.'

'You don't understand, Christie... Professor Fenwick is special... and I have my integrity as an engineer to think of. I can't knowingly participate in fraud.'

'That's all right then. Just don't know. You're foreign, how could they say you should have known?'

'But you've just made serious charges.'

'A bunch of drunken lies. No need to worry your rosary. Who'd believe Christie anyway? It's all stories. Everything is stories. If you want certainty take up a shell from the beach, put your ears to it and listen to what the ghost of the flesh that lived in it is telling you. What you hear might as well be the truth, the whole truth and nothing but the truth. Today I've been your shell, tomorrow you'll find another. Mr Curtis is blooming, Professor Fenwick is an honest priest, Rushton is the kind of manager that martyrs are made of; or else Mr Curtis is drowning in his own decomposition, Professor Fenwick is a practitioner of the black arts and Rushton is one of his altar boys. Pick whatever version of whatever story you prefer, it's all the same. You can't know anything in life for sure, you might as well make it up. If there was something like a leprechaun and he gave me three wishes, do you know what they'd be? I'd want out, out and out, that's God's truth I swear.'

'You mean to say there are no leprechauns?' I asked emptily, my mind dwelling on the allegations against Professor Fenwick.

'Of course there are no fucking leprechauns. Are you thick or what? What do you take the Irish for, a bunch of pissed primitives?' He sucked at the whiskey bottle defiantly. 'Look what the English leprechauns have done for you: fancy clothes, fancy words and fancy science. You've disappeared up the English cunt without knowing it. Me, I hold on to something else, even if I invent it. Call it Irishness if you want, call it anything, but at least I don't get sucked in. I'm still here, prick and all, and the cunt will have to drag me in screaming.'

I left him in this bleak mood and made my way back to the relative sanctuary of Mrs Rutherford's house. When I reached the poplar trees which marked the exit from his yard I looked back at the scene of disorder. From a safe distance his cottage had the appearance of a picturesque shambles, leaning to one side, tiles missing from the roof and gutters overhanging with moss. It was the kind of dwelling you'd imagine a hermit to be inhabiting, in an English fairy tale from one of my story-books. When I looked again I could see it for what it was – woodwormed, crippled with hatred, wanting to crash to the ground more catastrophically than the cliff's fall.

PART III

TWELVE

Winter came, Mrs Rutherford's garden withered and it was time to leave. I stayed indoors while she tended her stricken plants, not wanting to intrude on the privacy of her grief. She cut off all the summer growth from the shrubs, raked up fallen leaves and twigs. She was as scrupulous with the remains as she was when the garden bloomed. The compost heap swelled, the stench of the mulch carried the length of the garden into the house. I admired the faith with which she planted narcissi and tulip bulbs, hiding them in the soil as if hiding her surviving ornaments from thieves.

'You must be relieved it's all over,' she said, taking off her gardening gloves for the last time and rinsing them in the sink. I nodded, unable to say anything, out of a sadness for her. She put the kettle on. 'Jack will miss you,' she said, 'no more companionship for him except me. I think he's grown quite attached, you know how dogs are. He prefers you to me.' I looked at him lying warmly and complacently on his blanket between the two cupboards, feeling guilty that I had no affection for him. He was a stupid cruel dog, the smell of blood permanently on his breath. Still she cared for him, even when he kept digging up her precious bulbs, threatening to destroy the prospects of the next year's garden. 'He's not a man, he's only a dog, you can't blame him,' she said, taking each paw and slapping it in gentle reproach. She ruffled his ears and hugged him. I remained unconvinced that it was not done out of malice.

'You've completed what you set out to do. You saw the task through to the end. There's a kind of honourableness in that. Such honourableness makes up for everything else, don't you think?'

'How do you mean?'

'Well, whatever went on before is paid for, compensated, almost forgiven, something like that. Don't you look at your sea-wall and feel forgiven? Whatever you broke before or gave pain to no longer matters. Through one monumental act you caused the thousands of petty ones to disappear.'

'I'm not sure we can get rid of the past so instantly, if at all. Whatever you make afterwards is only some small amends, even if you spend the rest of your life piling one ten-ton rock upon another upon another until the heap of fifty thousand is laid out in a neat, almost innocent line. You're always drawn back to the memory of the original heap.'

'Where will you go from here?' she asked, sensing that I would be more comfortable talking about the future than the past.

'I'm not sure. I was planning to do some further studies with Professor Fenwick in London but I've decided to go home. There's always some emergency there that needs to be worked at. I'll have to see when I get there.'

'Whatever happens you can always come back. You know you'll always be at home here.' Embarrassed by her own sincerity, she immediately busied herself with the teapot and the laying-out of chocolate biscuits. 'There are enough emergencies in this garden to warrant your presence, I can tell you,' she said, her lightness of tone barely disguising a genuine sadness. 'I'll always need someone to mend the hose, to sharpen the scissors, to straighten the teeth of the fork and to ward off the birds. Christie was my handyman and scarecrow rolled into one until Jack and these masks drove him away.'

'Where's Jack now – your husband, I mean?' I asked for the last time, hoping to elicit some gothic confession from her. As soon as the question was uttered I regretted my impulsiveness in case it caused anxiety in her. I wished I could control my urge to pry, as Christie had cautioned.

She seemed unconcerned though by the question. 'As far as I know he really did return to Africa,' she said in a matter-of-fact voice. 'To tell the truth, when I'm by myself I never think of him being here or there. I seem to have put him out of my mind and buried him completely. He's a scent of smoke and a dropping of ash from the last cigarette he smoked in this house, which is all I remember or maybe care to remember. Of course there are other memories but he and they never rise to the surface – not until you ask. I must admit that since you've been around I've found myself daydreaming. I wonder why? Perhaps it's because you're a man. Why else would it be, since the two of you are so different in all other ways?'

The casual way in which she confessed his death in her mind disturbed me momentarily. 'Have you heard from him since? Has he never written you a letter since?' I continued to probe.

'He may or may not have done. To be honest, a year exactly after he left – August 6th 1972, around two p.m. – I went through the house, gathered up whatever of his belongings lingered here and there, and burnt them in the garden. It was the day of my independence. Come to think of it, your countrymen got theirs from the English in the same year, didn't they?' She paused to work out the new connection she had made between us.

'I was nearly sixteen then, at the beginning of adulthood,' I said, startled by the coincidence that had eventually drawn me to her.

'Anyway, I spaded the ash around the cherry tree which he had planted when we first moved in as a married couple. He said the tree would be for us, it would blossom and grow and outlive us and always be here. The kind of speech that African nationalists make on independence, planting some commemorative tree, before proceeding to rake their treasury and muck up their country. Many times after Jack had gone I had a mind to chop the tree down, but it was only for the sake of the fruit that I left it alone. It's the healthiest tree in the garden, giving hundreds of cherries a year. So I did the next best thing and fed it his remains.' A look of spite crossed her face which she could not maintain for long, being too generous in nature. 'Anyway, I'm sure the sea-wall will summon you back here in a few years' time. It'll need constant repairing wouldn't it?'

'Maintenance, but not repairing I shouldn't think, not for a decade at least.'

'I'm not sure… it does look a bit shorter than I imagined it would be. I wonder how well it will stand up to twenty-foot waves?'

'How do you mean, shorter?' I asked in an alarmed voice, remembering Christie's charge that insufficient rocks had been delivered.

'I didn't mean to make you panic,' she apologised, mistaking my anxiety for wounded pride, 'it looks solid enough and I wouldn't want to doubt the professionalism of all involved.'

Later that afternoon, before it grew dark, I went down to the beach to inspect the wall for the final time. It stretched for half a mile, curving with the contour of the shore. It looked distinctly out of place on the empty beach, obviously placed there by human effort. Everything else was made by sea and wind; the rocks piled upon each other so hastily, intruded on the timeless barrenness of the place. Coils of rotting rope, the odd plank of wood, shells, pieces of bone – the sea had washed them in and would wash them out again, each tide bringing in a haul of predictable debris. The wall of granite disturbed this timeless rhythm of depositing and shifting. It settled monumentally and unnaturally in the sand, refusing to budge. It bore all the traits of the humans who had placed it there. It suddenly looked monstrous and cruel, stubborn and brutishly arrogant, an awesome deformity. I regretted that I had made it and half wished that the sea would breach it, break it down to meek pebbles.

'You must be proud of your work, the solidity of it,' Mrs Rutherford suggested, trying on this final evening's conversation to summarise the meaning of my stay with her.

'I am,' I answered uneasily. Would it last, I wondered, given the doubts about the actual quantity of rocks used; and would I want it to last?

'You are as privileged as any sculptor. You've shaped something in stone which will be here for a long time, if not for ever. And you've done it in England, so you've carved your name in our history.'

'It'll eventually disappear into the sea or else it will be replaced by some other engineering works.'

'Don't be so bashful,' she scolded me, 'you should rejoice in the visibility of your handiwork. Rejoice!'

I was invisible to the village, wall or no wall, I thought to myself, suddenly resenting the way they had viewed me, or rather not viewed me. It was decent of Mrs Rutherford to claim that I now belonged to the heritage of England, but I knew that I had only been a transient worker, like the Irishman Christie. I could appreciate his sullenness, his subdued rage, his desire to smash things. The wall I helped to make would be acknowledged for a moment but I would soon be washed out of their memories. Future generations would see the wall as something that was always there, a quintessentially English monument; the efforts of Christie and myself would be erased by ignorance or national sentiment. Was it not always thus in England: the drift into a deliberate unconsciousness; any awakening being a jolt of patriotic sentiment? Mrs Rutherford herself, on one of our trips to Hastings, had pointed me to a splendid mansion in the Georgian style. 'To think that West-Indian slave money built that,' she said, 'but the crowds who go to gape at the fine furniture and fine paintings think it's the best of English heritage. And the guidebooks don't tell them any different.'

Did I want to be visible though? Did I not break the four lights so as to remain in darkness? Did not Mr Curtis tire of flashbulbs in his face, spurn the company of sympathisers and seek out the obscurity of his own self? He was not dying of anything as sentimental as a broken heart. I wanted to believe that he had come to realise the monstrosity of his imagination, the monstrosity of his ambition to build Aswan dams in the guise of patriotism. He had come to realise that England was a small place with small people; everything had been shrinking since his birth in the 1920s, when one colony after another agitated for independence. After the collapse of his mission he withdrew into a private space, wanting to forget the history that had awakened huge ambition in him; a history that had ceased to exist in glory but still provoked a nostalgia for the monumental. If he was mourning, as Christie claimed, it was a masquerade of grief, like a prophet weeping over Jerusalem. Mrs Rutherford too had withdrawn into singularity, but less securely, for my presence stirred desires in her which she had genuinely sought to bury. Above all she still wanted to retaliate, but acts of retaliation were bound to be gestures of masquerade, for England had long ceased to matter. To smash up England would be no more than going berserk in a waxwork museum. It would be a waste of action. And yet she twitched constantly with anger, unable to emancipate herself from history. I could leave both of them and return home. Guyana had its own legacies of deceit and cruelty, but there was space to forget. The land was vast and empty enough to encourage new beginnings in obscure corners. I had to believe this, otherwise there would be nowhere to go and nothing to do but act out ritual public disputes.

'I'll be alone when you're gone,' Mrs Rutherford said, reading my desire for obscurity, 'and I'm almost looking forward to it.'

'I hope I wasn't too much of an interruption.'

'You were a terrible interruption...' Her eyes lit up with typical mischief. 'For a start I'll have to get used to drinking on my own. When I first got Jack I poured some in his bowl. He lapped it up out of greed and then started to cough and vomit. He behaved badly for hours afterwards, leaping at me. At least you were a gentleman! Come on, let's drink a last toast.' She went to the cabinet and poured out two large glasses. 'Here's to gentlemen, wherever they may be,' she said and, not waiting for me, swallowed all her wine in one go. She held the empty glass and looked at the fireplace as if contemplating tossing it there in utter contempt or utter regret.

We sat in silence in the waiting-room. Our conversations had truly ended. She looked haggard and irritable, her eyes puffed up from lack of sleep. She wanted the train to come quickly so that she could retreat back to the familiarity of her world. The winter ahead would be long and silent. Banished from her garden she would stay indoors, wrapped in layers of clothing. She would look out of her window at the desolation of frost and growling wind, at all the dead twigs and stumps of interrupted growth. She would outwait the season, out of custom, out of stubbornness, until the sun appeared again and plants twitched to life in the garden. She knew exactly which bulbs would sprout from the ground first, she knew the exact spot where they would break through, and she was intent on keeping alive and awake to witness their birth.

Five minutes before the train departed she opened her handbag. She fished out the string of pearls we had seen in the shop window at Hastings. 'This is for your mother,' she said, 'you were right. I'm too elderly for them.' Her mood softened as she pressed them into my hand. I wished I had something precious to give her in return. I wished I had brought to England one of the Dutch bottles I had dug up, but she would only have put it to her nose and smelt the rottenness of past ages. 'You saved my home and my garden by your sea-wall, that's gift enough,' she said, forgiving my empty-handedness.

When the train pulled out I searched my pocket for cigarettes and felt something odd. I eased it out: the head of the flower I had picked by the wayside on my first day at work. Forgotten in my pocket, it had dried and grown flat, yet still retaining some of its violent colour. I held it carefully in the cup of my hand, appalled that the slightest movement could cause it to flake and disappear.

ALSO BY DAVID DABYDEEN

Slave Song   ISBN: 978 1 84523 004 3, 72pp, £7.99

Slave Song is unquestionably one of the most important collections of Caribbean/Black British poetry published in the last thirty years. On its first publication in 1984 it won the Commonwealth Poetry Prize.

At the heart of *Slave Song* are the voices of African slaves and Indian labourers expressing, in a Guyanese Creole that is as far removed from Standard English as is possible, their songs of defiance, of a thwarted erotic energy. But surrounding this harsh and lyrical core of Creole expression is an elaborate critical apparatus of translations (which deliberately reveal the actual untranslatability of the Creole) and a parody of the kind of critical commentary that does no more than paraphrase or at best contextualise the original poem. Here, Dabydeen is engaged in a play of masks, an expression of his own duality and a critique of the relationship which is at the core of Caribbean writing: that between the articulate writer and the supposedly voiceless workers and peasants.

This new edition has an afterword by David Dabydeen that briefly explores his response to these poems after more than twenty years.

Turner   ISBN: 978 1 90071 568 3, 84pp, £7.99

David Dabydeen's "Turner" is a long narrative poem written in response to JMW Turner's celebrated painting "Slavers Throwing Overboard the Dead & Dying". Dabydeen's poem focuses on what is hidden in Turner's painting, the submerged head of the drowning African. In inventing a biography and the drowned man's unspoken desires, including the resisted temptation to fabricate an idyllic past, the poem brings into confrontation the wish for renewal and the inescapable stains of history, including the meaning of Turner's painting.

"A major poem, full of lyricism and compassion, which gracefully shoulders the burden of history and introduces us to voices from the past whose voices we have all inherited" – Caryl Phillips

The Intended   ISBN: 978 1 84523 013 5, 246pp, £8.99

The narrator of *The Intended* is twelve when he leaves his village in rural Guyana to come to England. There he is abandoned into social care, but seizes every opportunity to follow his aunt's farewell advice: "...but you must tek education...pass plenty exam." With a scholarship to Oxford, and an upper-class white fiancée, he has unquestionably arrived, but at the cost of ignoring the other part of his aunt's farewell: "you is we, remember you is we." First published almost fifteen years ago, *The Intended*'s portrayal of the instability of identity and relations between whites, African-Caribbeans and Asians in South London is as contemporary and pertinent as ever. As an Indian from Guyana, the narrator is seen as a "Paki" by the English, and as some mongrel hybrid by "real" Asians from India and Pakistan; as sharing a common British "Blackness" whilst acutely conscious of the real cultural divisions between Africans and Indians back in Guyana. At one level a moving semi-autobiographical novel, *The Intended* is also a sophisticated postcolonial text with echoes of *Heart of Darkness*.

The Counting House   ISBN: 978 1 84523 015 9, 180pp, £8.99

Set in the early nineteenth century, *The Counting House* follows the lives of Rohini and Vidia, a young married couple struggling for survival in a small, caste-ridden Indian village who are seduced by the recruiter's talk of easy work and plentiful land if they sign up as indentured labourers to go to British Guiana. There, however, they discover a harsh fate as "bound coolies" in a country barely emerging from the savage brutalities of slavery. Having abandoned their families and a country that seems increasingly like a paradise, they must come to terms with their problematic encounters with an Afro-Guyanese population hostile to immigrant labour, with rebels such as Kampta who has made an early abandonment of Indian village culture, and confront the truths of their uprooted condition.

Our Lady of Demerara   ISBN: 9781845230692; pp. 288; £9.99

Drama critic Lance Yardley is only 30 but is already a seedy wreck of a man, spending his nights in the back streets of Coventry looking for prostitutes. A working-class boy brought up in a broken home on a council estate, he has sought escape in literature and through his marriage to an actress, the great-granddaughter of a 19th-century Englishman who made his fortune from the sugar plantations in Guyana. At first Elizabeth attracts Yardley, but their differences of class exacerbate the mutual hatred that grows between them. Later he is drawn to a mysterious Indian girl, Rohini. She seems shy, but sells her body to customers when her boss goes out of town. When she dies suddenly, the victim of a strange and violent assassin, Yardley decides to decamp abroad for a while. He goes to Guyana, not least because he wants to learn more about an Irish priest who as an old man has been a priest in Coventry, but as a young man had worked as a missionary in Guyana. The priest's fragmented journals seem to offer Yardley some possible answers to his own spiritual malaise, but the Guyana he discovers provokes more questions than answers.

Johnson's Dictionary   ISBN: 9781845232184; pp. 221; £9.99

In a novel that might be dreamed or remembered by Manu, a revenant from Dabydeen's epic poem, "Turner", we meet slaves, lowly women on the make, lustful overseers, sodomites and pious Jews, characters who have somehow come alive from engravings by Hogarth and others. Hogarth himself turns up as a drunkard official artist in Demerara, from whom the slave Cato steals his skills and discovers a way of remaking his world. The transforming power of words is what enlightens Francis when his master gifts him a copy of *Johnson's Dictionary*, whilst the idiot savant, known as Mmadboy, reveals the uncanny mathematical skills that enable him to beat Adam Smith to the discovery of the laws of capital accumulation. From the dens of sexual specialities where the ex-slave Francis conducts a flagellant mission to cure his clients of their man-love (and preach abolition), to the sugar estates of Demerara, Dabydeen's novel revels in the connections of Empire, Art, Literature and human desire.

Ed. Kevin Grant
The Art of David Dabydeen ISBN: 978 1 90071 510 2, 231pp, £12.99

In this volume, leading scholars discuss Dabydeen's poetry and fiction in the context of the politics and culture of Britain and the Caribbean. The essays explore his concern with the plurality of Caribbean experience; the dislocation of slavery and indenture; migration and the consequent divisions in the Caribbean psyche. In particular, the focus is on Dabydeen's aesthetic practice as a consciously post-colonial writer; his exploration of the contrasts between rural creole and standard English; the power of language to subvert accepted realities; his use of multiple masks as ways of dealing with issues of identity; and the play of destabilizing techniques within his narrative strategies.

Eds Lynne Macedo and Kampta Karran
No Land, No Mother: Essays on the Work of David Dabydeen
ISBN: 978 1 84523 020 3, 236pp, £12.99

Essays by Aleid Fokkema, Tobias Döring, Heike Härting and Madina Tlostanova provide rewardingly complex readings of Dabydeen's *Turner*, locating it within a revived tradition of Caribbean epic. Lee Jenkins and Pumla Gqola explore Dabydeen's fondness for intertextual reference, his dialogue with canonic authority and ideas about the masculine. Michael Mitchell, Mark Stein, Christine Pagnoulle and Gail Low focus on his more recent fiction. Looking more closely at Dabydeen's Indo-Guyanese background, this collection complements the earlier *The Art of David Dabydeen*.

All available on-line from www.peepaltreepress.com